THE SWORD OF LIFE

Dave Morris

To Oliver

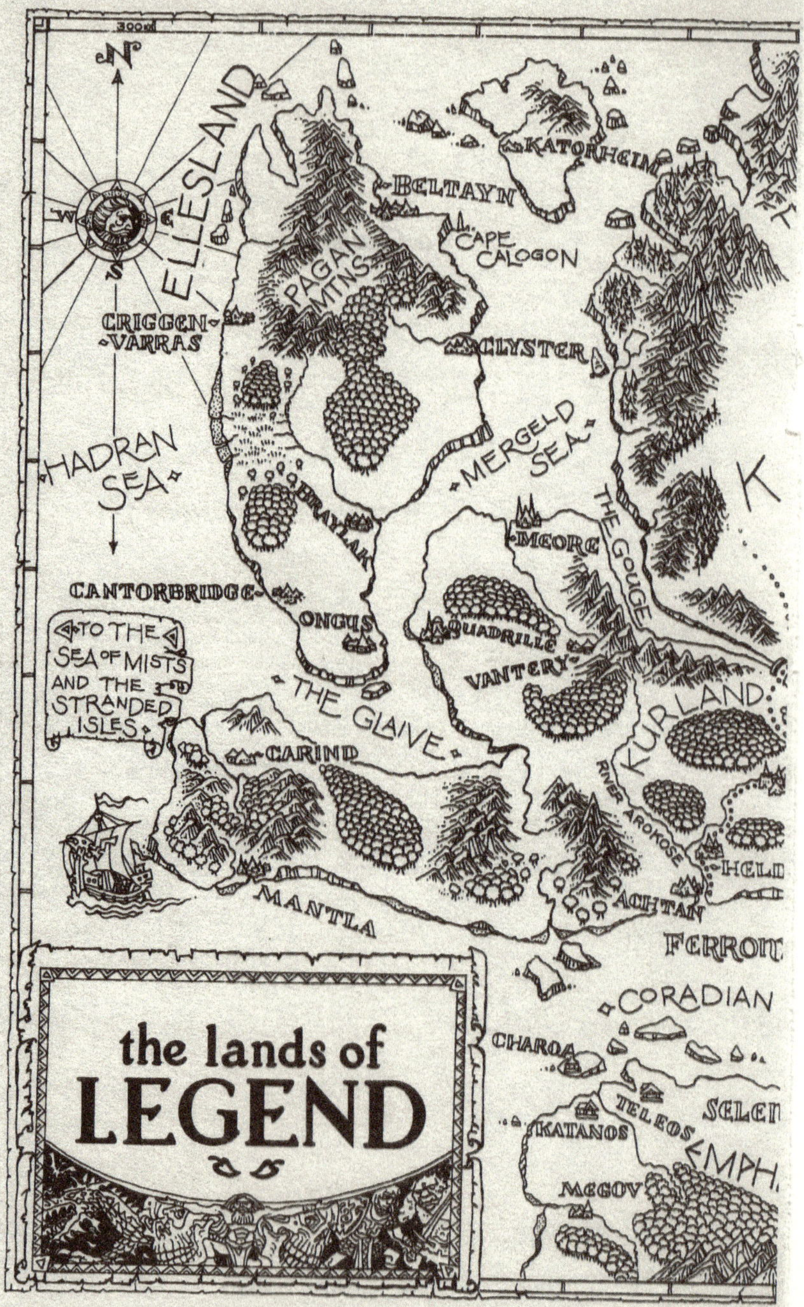
300ml
N
W E
S
ELLESLAND
KATORHEIM
BELTAYN
CAPE CALOGON
PAGAN MTNS
CRIGGEN-VARRAS
CLYSTER
MERGELD SEA
HADRAN SEA
THE GOUGE
K
MEORC
BRAYAH
QUADRILLE
CANTORBRIDGE
ONGUS
VANTERY
TO THE SEA OF MISTS AND THE STRANDED ISLES
KURLAND
THE GLAIVE
CARIND
RIVER AROKOSE
HELD
MANTLA
ACHTAN
FERROIT
CORADIAN
CHAROA
SELEI
KATANOS
TELEOS
EMPH
MEGOV
the lands of
LEGEND

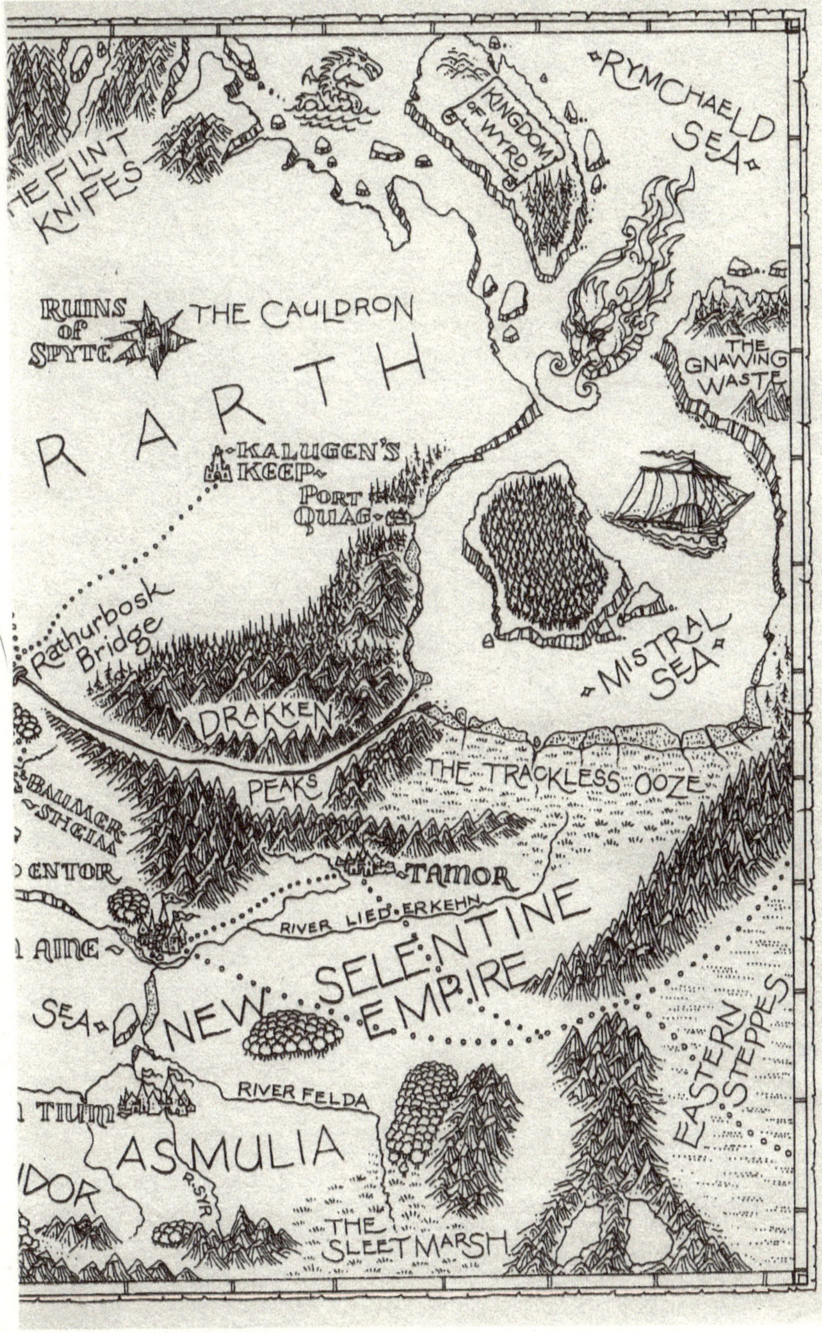

THE FLINT KNIFES
RYMCHAELD SEA
KINGDOM OF WYRD
RUINS of SPYTE
THE CAULDRON
RARTH
THE GNAWING WASTE
KALUGEN'S KEEP
PORT QUAG
Rathurbosk Bridge
MISTRAL SEA
DRAKKEN
PEAKS
THE TRACKLESS OOZE
BALMER SHEIM
ENTOR
TAMOR
RIVER LIED ERKEHN
AINE
NEW SELENTINE EMPIRE
SEA
TIUM
EASTERN STEPPES
RIVER FELDA
ASMULIA
R. SYR
IDOR
THE SLEET MARSH

THE MAGI

Now as at all times I can see in the mind's eye,
In their stiff, painted clothes, the pale unsatisfied
ones
Appear and disappear in the blue depths of the sky
With all their ancient faces like rain-beaten stones,
And all their helms of silver hovering side by side,
And all their eyes still fixed, hoping to find once
more,
Being by Calvary's turbulence unsatisfied,
The uncontrollable mystery on the bestial floor.

W. B. Yeats

One:

The Pommel Stone

The old woman hunched over the cards, her breath a misty plume in the chill evening air. Beside her, the campfire crackled and spat sparks up to the grey sky. Altor waited patiently, smiling to himself as he saw the look of intense concentration darken the woman's wrinkled brow. When she looked up she was not smiling.

'This is an irresistible fate,' she said, gesturing at the cards. 'Your destiny is sealed by the Norns themselves. You will undertake some great task, a quest of tremendous importance.'

Touching a card with one thin brown hand, she went on: 'From the first card, which is the focus of the reading, the quest will involve the setting to right of some ancient ill. Another interpretation is that you will repair something that has been broken.'

'Perhaps the tiles on the monastery roof need fixing again,' said Altor flippantly, but the old woman ignored him.

'The Knave here suggests one you shall soon meet. A friend or companion, perhaps. The next card suggests that a long journey lies ahead of you, and the surrounding cards indicate great hardships to be endured along the way. This card, the Hosts of Yeth, shows that those obstacles will be both many and dangerous. Powerful forces will oppose you. Turning to the next card, we see your near future. The Archon, icy of gaze and stern of countenance. A ruler, or at any rate a man who expects to be obeyed. If your quest is not in his interests then you can count on him to oppose you. But take heart, young man, for here beside him is the card we call the Wise Mother. She is the feminine principle—the gentle dreams bidden by lullabies, of tales told by a warm hearth, selfless love and the comforting word.'

Altor had been listening with amused scepticism, but the woman's words awoke an old sorrow. Raised by monks from early childhood, he had no memory of his own parents.

The old woman gathered the cards and began to shuffle them, meeting Altor's sad gaze with her dark sunken eyes. 'The Knave, who came first, is a stark contrast indeed to the Archon, and you noticed that their faces on the cards were turned away from each other? Though some will oppose you, the cards seem to say, you may find one to be your friend.'

Altor shrugged and got to his feet, stretching his broad shouldered frame in a massive yawn. 'If you say so.' He dropped two silver coins into the old woman's hand. The firelight made them blaze like droplets of blood, reflected in the dark pools of her eyes.

Night was darkening the sky and closing a wall of blackness around the campfires. Altor had joined a number of other wayfarers who for mutual protection had banded together to travel through the great forest of southern Krarth. A pilgrim who had been waiting nearby, seeing that the fortune-teller was finished with Altor, came hurrying over to learn what the cards said about his own destiny. Pondering the meaning of the old woman's prophecy, Altor walked away across the clearing, which was now bustling with activity as merchants, hunters and pilgrims prepared camp for the night.

In the time since Altor had sat down for his card-reading, some foresters had appeared with their families and were now roasting haunches of venison on a spit. Altor sniffed the aroma of the meat longingly, but in the cook pot over his own campfire simmered only a thin broth of roots and herbs. He hunkered down beside it and poured himself a bowl, regretting the two coins he had given the soothsayer which might have been better spent to buy a loaf of bread and a slice of venison.

The plangent notes of a melancholy tune drifted across the clearing. Altor looked over to see a man strumming a lyre. He wore a tunic and breeches of cotton that had once been white, perhaps, but now were travel-stained and grey. As he sipped his broth, Altor studied the man's strong proud face, idly wondering what had brought him to this desolate spot. The wistful melody he played was nothing like the ballads and jaunty jigs of a typical minstrel. Impelled by curiosity, Altor strolled over to listen to the music.

The musician looked up as Altor approached. He saw a big youth in the simple homespun tunic of a warrior-monk. In the months Altor had been travelling, his close cropped hair had grown into a corn-coloured broom on top of his wide brow, and combined with his earnest expression and honest yeoman's face it made him look intimidating and comical in equal measure.

Without ceasing to play, the musician smiled and said, 'I noticed you getting your fortune told. Anything interesting?'

Altor laughed self-consciously. 'She claimed to foresee a stirring destiny for me. It sounded just the thing for a hero, but I'm afraid that in this case the cards must have got mixed up.'

The musician nodded as he plucked the strings of his lyre. 'The monks of your order are warriors, though. Don't you like the idea of being a hero, lad?'

Altor reddened, not sure if the man was teasing him. 'I had a letter for Brother Emeritus, one of the sages of our sect. Having delivered it, I'm now on my way back to Osterlin Abbey, in Ellesland. It's not my duty to go off involving myself in mysterious quests, even if any came along.'

Altor waited, but the musician had nothing more to say. He seemed lost in his oddly poignant melody. Altor looked past him to the edge of the clearing, where a circle of foresters wrapped in long grey travelling cloaks were peering intently at a game of Krarthian chequers being played by two tall men. The chequers players hunched over the board, which they had placed on a flat stone between them. Patting their hands to stave off the chill, they crouched like dire wolves in their mantles of blue-grey fur, so engrossed in their game as to be oblivious of the onlookers.

The rules of Krarthian chequers differed from the version played in Altor's homeland, but he understood enough to follow the basic moves. Instilled with a warrior's training, he found the military precision of the game fascinating and, forgetting the musician, drifted over for a closer look. The players had deployed their pieces across the board like two generals sending forth troops to battle, so it was with surprise that Altor saw one of them abruptly move a piece into a position where it was swiftly taken. A cunning trap, he wondered, designed to lure the opponent into a costly exchange of pieces? But no, the other player swiftly captured several pieces without risk.

Soon, as night settled over the forest, the game ended. With the white counters forced together in the middle of the board, the player controlling the black pieces surrounded and eliminated them all.

As each piece was taken, one of the onlookers would lose interest in the game and, turning, go back to his bedroll. Altor, absorbed in the game, failed to notice this until the last white piece was swept away and he looked up to find he was the only spectator left.

The two fur-cloaked players rose and nodded curtly to each other. Neither winner nor loser showed any emotion. Altor wondered if this was because of sportsmanship or sheer indifference.

'I'd like a game,' he said, 'if either of you gentlemen would care to explain the moves.'

They ignored him, packing up the board and pieces without even giving him a glance. Altor was left alone to watch them walk away through the flickering orange glow of the camp fires.

A sense of unease gnawed at him. There was something odd about the game, and something very sinister about the foresters themselves. Or then again, it might just be his imagination... Altor shook his head irritably. The abbot had believed him mature enough to be entrusted with this mission. He was ashamed at himself for getting spooked by the loneliness of the spot and the unfriendliness of strangers. He strode back and fed some more wood to the fire before climbing inside his sleeping bag.

All around the clearing, the sounds of talk and laughter gradually faded as people turned in for the night. But, much to his annoyance, Altor found that sleep would not come. He shut his eyes, but the sounds of the crackling fires and the sighing of wind in the pines remained to disrupt the stillness of the night.

Suddenly he sat bolt upright, every nerve in his body tense. Just on the verge of sleep, a sudden thought had startled him back to wakefulness. Staring around the clearing in the dull gleam of the campfires, he saw now what he had failed to notice before. The pilgrims and ordinary travellers were arranged as the white pieces had been in the chequers game. The fur-clad foresters who had watched the game had placed themselves around the perimeter of the clearing in the same deployment used by the black pieces just before the game had reached its sudden end.

Cursing himself for a fool, Altor snatched his sword from its scabbard and jumped to his feet. That was why the chequers players hadn't cared about the outcome of their game—they hadn't really been playing at all, they had been planning their attack! A cry of warning whipcracked from Altor's lips even as he bounded across the clearing towards the spot where the two chequers players lay. Whatever skulduggery was afoot, those two were obviously the ringleaders.

The nearest of the two started to rise with a growl. Quick as he was, Altor was quicker. He planted his sword-point at the man's throat and met his glare of furious hatred with a stolid look. Behind, the other man crouched like an animal at bay.

'It's past your bed-time, isn't it?' said Altor in a level tone. 'Planning some mischief?'

'What's going on?' a voice called blearily across the clearing. 'Keep it down, can't you? Some of us are trying to sleep.'

The chequers player deliberately leaned forward so that the tip of Altor's blade pricked his skin. A tiny bead of blood formed at his throat. Then he drew back, and at once the wound closed. As Altor stared in astonishment the man smiled, baring long canine teeth that filled his mouth.

'We are not as you,' said the other, edging forward. 'We are night's brood, the brothers of wolves...'

'Werewolves!'

Altor threw himself backwards. He acted not a moment too soon. Unconcerned by the steel sword that was powerless to harm him, the first werewolf brought his hand up in a scything cut. Talons slashed at thin air. The attack would have ripped out the young warrior-monk's bowels if he'd been a fraction slower.

The commotion had roused one or two of the sleeping travellers nearby. They woke just in time to see some of the fur clad foresters leaning over them, then long knives snuffed out their lives.

Altor, rolling across the ground, flung aside his sword and instead pulled a burning log from the fire. One of the werewolves barked an order and a group of the silent foresters loped forward to the attack. Altor thrust the burning brand into the nearest man's face and, as he reeled back with a scream, pushed him onto the knives of the others. Blood spurted in the firelight. Altor nodded to himself with grim satisfaction. Even if he couldn't slay the werewolves themselves, at least the foresters who served them were not immune to death.

A cold metallic light now crept across the scene. Glancing aside, Altor saw the rising disc of the Blue Moon, one of the five swift comets that swept the skies of Krarth. As its beams struck the two chequers players, they began to transform. Hair bristled on their hands and feet, their faces stretched to the shape of vulpine snouts. They dropped to all fours as the fur spread across their bodies. Slavering jaws spilled hot saliva on the frosty grass as they fixed their eyes on Altor. Then, raising their muzzles to the Blue Moon, they gave vent to long horrifying howls of murderous intent.

It was a chilling sound, and more than enough to rouse any of the travellers who had not already woken. Some screamed and caught up their belongings, intending to flee. The foresters fell on them swiftly, slashing with their long knives. Some of the pilgrims took up cudgels and quarterstaves, determined to fight to the last.

The night was split by roars of anguish, the moans of the injured, the screams of the dying. Altor struck at one of the silent foresters, catching him across the brow, and the man fell in a shower of red sparks. Another came charging forward with a loud cry. Before he could reach him, Altor wrestled the knife from the fallen man's hand and flung it to impale the other in the throat. He collapsed across the body of his comrade.

Altor planted himself with his back to one of the campfires so that he could not be outflanked. Flailing desperately to right and left with the burning brand, he managed to hold his foes at bay. Soon, seeing no way past the young warrior's guard, the werewolves' henchmen fell back. Altor took advantage of the respite to look how the others were faring. Some of the pilgrims had fallen, others were fleeing into the gloomy depths of the forest. A brave few still fought on as he did. Further away, on the other side of the clearing, a group of Kurlish traders were rallying their hired guards to attempt a charge.

Another adversary lunged close, almost taking Altor unawares. The man ducked under the arc of fire from the swinging brand, but Altor twisted aside and smashed the heel of his left hand against the man's jaw, sending him sprawling. Even as he fought, part of Altor's mind had time to wonder why the werewolves had attacked. Not merely for the traders' gold, surely? More likely for the sake of wholesale slaughter, but that too was strange. Normal wolves preferred to pick off solitary prey rather than choosing a battle where they would be outnumbered.

He looked around for the werewolves themselves. There was one—a great hunched shape with eyes that blazed balefully in the dark. It was crouching over a fallen figure and gore ran freely from its jaws, black like oil in the dim light of the Blue Moon. Altor heard its snarling voice as it called to its brother, and by concentrating he could make out the distorted words of its speech.

'He does not have the stone,' it said.

The other werewolf prowled nearer, gave the corpse a sidelong glance. 'He has hidden it. No matter—he will never get to find it now.'

'Our work is done, then,' growled the first. 'Come!'

The last word rose in a long eerie howl. At once the fur cloaked foresters paused and fell back, turning to follow their werewolf masters into the forest. In moments they had been swallowed up by darkness. Altor and the survivors of the travelling band stood dumbstruck amid the carnage.

Despite his youth, Altor was the first to recover from the shock. 'Check the wounded,' he said to the leader of the Kurlish traders. 'Use torn blankets to staunch the bleeding. You,' he added, pointing to one of the pilgrims, 'you have a bag of herbal remedies, I believe? If they're at all effective you'd better fetch them now.'

The mercenaries whom the traders relied on to protect their wares had done little during the fighting, too stunned to do much more then grab their swords and shields. Now their captain came forward and offered to organize a search of the surrounding forest. 'We need to round up those who fled or they'll die of exposure,' he said.

Altor was on the point of joining the search party when he noticed a feeble stirring from the werewolves' savaged victim. There was a groan and, stooping, he recognized the musician he had spoken to earlier. 'Don't move,' he said. 'I'll get help.'

The man stared at him from a face as white as clay. His eyes were fiery with pain. 'I'm beyond any help,' he gasped. 'But they didn't get the stone...'

His voice trailed off momentarily as blood came bubbling to his lips. Altor, who had been trained in all aspects of warfare, recognized that death was near. He did not try to delude the man. 'It's true you're dying. Tell me your name; I'll see you get a decent burial.'

The man stared back and then, mustering the last of his strength, struggled to a half-sitting position. 'Haversack...' he muttered. Altor saw it lying nearby and put it into the man's hands. Reaching painfully inside, he took out a parcel wound with velvet cloth. His hands stained the velvet as he unwrapped what lay within. It was his lyre.

Altor thought that the man intended it to be buried with him, but suddenly he began to pound it against the frost-hardened ground. Altor saw that the effort was causing him agony and tried to gently take it from him, but the man was determined. On the third attempt, the base of the lyre broke open and a round glittering object rolled out.

Altor picked it up. It was a magnificent jewel that sparkled with inner light, catching the blue moonbeams and the red glow of the fires and transmuting them into a blaze of vivid colours.

'The Five are gathering power...' gasped the dying man, somehow finding the strength to raise himself on one elbow as he spoke his last words. 'Soon they'll return to the world. Only the swords can stop them—the Sword of Life and the Sword of Death. That gem is from the pommel of the Sword of Life. You must find the other pieces.'

Altor was dismayed. 'I pray you, do not charge me with this quest. I am not free to undertake it. I have other responsibilities.'

The man's breath came unevenly, his eyes clouding as he sank back to the ground. 'You must... You must stop the Five...'

'Who?' Altor shook his head. He did not like to refuse a dying man's request, but his first duty was to return to Osterlin Abbey. 'There must be somebody else. Tell me who to give the gem to—I can do that much.'

The man's voice was so weak that Altor had to strain to catch his words: 'Take the pommel stone to Kalugen's Keep. Give it to Janirus. Then you'll know.'

He said no more but gave a deep groan and went limp, his eyes freezing in the sightlessness of death, still fixed imploringly on Altor's face.

Altor rose to his feet. He was torn. Duty required him to return without delay to his abbey. Honour demanded that he carry out the dead man's final wishes.

Suddenly the choice was simple. 'Very well,' he muttered grimly to the night wind, 'I'll go to Kalugen's Keep.'

Two:

Kalugen's Keep

The Keep of Magus Kalugen stood in the heart of the icy plains of Krarth, a monolithic citadel of black stone beneath skies that were blue, cloudless and cold. The monotony of the surrounding landscape was relieved only by the occasional stunted willow tree growing beside muddy ponds. The Keep itself dwarfed all around it, like a tumble of dark rocks that had fallen from the heavens.

As Altor approached the towering walls, a bitter wind blew across the sere grass of the marshes and sent sluggish ripples through the puddles of mire that occupied the hollows. He was anxious to complete his task, hand the pommel stone on to the one the musician had named, and quit this forbidding place. It would be best not to waste any time. In only a matter of weeks the marsh waters would begin to rise, drowning the land and the causeways leading to the citadel. Then Kalugen's Keep would be shut off from the outside world for another year. No one would enter or leave in that time except for the magi who ruled the land of Krarth, borne on their flying carpets. Only in mid-year would the citizens of the Keep be allowed to emerge and sow their fields with straggle-wheat before the harsh winter once more set in.

Jostling through the gabbling throng of merchants and peasants pouring along the causeway, Altor entered the massive gate. The colossal grey stone blocks were like the maw of a hungry demon, its teeth the iron spikes of the open portcullis. Ahead stood sentries armed with pikes. Big surly men, they glared at Altor as though he were a notorious criminal or a carrier of plague, but once he had paid the gate toll they waved him through into the city without another glance.

Inside, the streets were narrow cobbled lanes lined with shuttered grey buildings. Altor had expected as much, Kalugen's Keep having a grim reputation. To his surprise, however, the whole city was festooned with multi-coloured flags which belied its dour semblance and gave it an almost festive air.

Somebody barged into Altor from behind and an eloquently acid insult was flung at his back. He turned to find himself face-to face with a young man of about his own age. That was the only thing they had in common. Although he had a sword at his hip, the other was not bulkily muscled like Altor but had an acrobat's trim physique. And his clothes were not the rough homespun of any common traveller. Even his boots, though he had obviously worn them for many leagues, were as fine as any southern courtier's, with their silver buckles and miniver lining. He wore pantaloons of gold velvet and a waistcoat studded with purple and red stones over a loose cream silk shirt fastened at the collar by a fire opal set in a silver clasp. His hooded cloak glittered like coal in the bleached daylight and his long black hair was swept back and bound in a pony tail under a jaunty hunting-cap set off with a single white peacock feather.

It was the peacock feather that struck Altor as most appropriate. He leaned down towards the young dandy and listened impassively as he finished his tirade.

'...you fog-witted yokel, can't you watch where you're going?'

Altor chuckled. 'Sorry, but wasn't it you that bumped into me?'

'What else do you expect, if you stand in the city's main thoroughfare gawping at your surroundings like a puppy in a boneyard?'

A group of merchants with heavily laden pack mules were just now entering the city, so both Altor and his new acquaintance were forced to move down the avenue into the main square. Here Altor noticed a booth set on a raised platform behind a rack bearing three splendidly-coloured coats of arms.

The press of traffic into the square carried them both over towards the platform. A man with a long nose and longer beard emerged from the booth and peered critically down at Altor's companion. 'Ho, fellow. Yes, I mean you. Our lord the magi seek champions. Did you wish to apply for the post?'

The dandy swirled back his cloak with a raffish gesture. 'Of course not.'

The man nodded. 'I thought as much. In that case, kindly move away from the front of the booth. Your costume is liable to distract people's attention from the magi's banners.'

The dandy spluttered in indignation but, unable to think of a suitable retort, strode off into the crowd. The bearded man was on the point of withdrawing into the booth when Altor caught his eye. He gave the young warrior a long thoughtful look. 'Perhaps you should consider becoming a champion, lad—assuming you aren't just some farmer's boy who stole that sword.'

'This sword is my own,' retorted Altor, 'and I know how to use it. But I am confused by all this talk of champions. Don't the magi of Krarth have men-at-arms aplenty to serve them?'

'I see you are a stranger to these parts. Otherwise you would know that every thirteen lunar months the magi converge here for their great contest. Each appoints one or more champions to descend into the Battlepits. The winner is he who returns from the underworld bearing the Emblem of Victory.'

'What do the magi stand to gain from such a contest?' asked Altor.

'Some say it's just a game for them, others that the magus whose champion wins the contest gains a tribute of gold and magic from all the others. All I can tell you for sure, lad, is that if you become a champion you'll never want for anything again.'

'I'm not interested in such a reward,' said Altor. 'I have to get back to my monastery in Ellesland. I only came to Kalugen's Keep so I could give this—'

He patted his money pouch, feeling for the pommel stone, and suddenly his heart ran with ice.

'It's gone!' Altor stared white-face back towards the gate. 'I must have dropped it when I paid the entrance toll...' He took three steps back across the square, then stopped and shook his head helplessly. 'I'll never find it.'

The bearded man clicked his tongue. 'Valuable, was it, this thing you lost?'

Altor shrugged. 'It's not that. I swore I'd bring it to someone in the city. I'd better go to the police barracks. Maybe somebody found it and handed it in.'

'The barracks! You could wait there forever for an honest militiaman to turn up,' said the man cynically. 'If anyone in the Keep found your treasure, lad, you can bet it's snug in their pocket. Failing that it'll be trodden under a foot of mire and slush. Take my advice and forget about it.'

Altor stared at him in amazement. 'Forget my sworn oath? How can you say such a thing? There must be something I can do.'

'Well...' The man tugged at his beard. 'I can't see how you could find your property now with anything less than sorcery. And, although there is much sorcery in the Keep, it is all in the hands of the magi.'

'Then I must ask a magus to help me.'

'The magi don't concern themselves with ordinary mortals, lad. You'd have as much luck praying to God for a silver florin to turn up in the next loaf of bread you buy.'

Almost beside himself with dismay, Altor stared around the square. Then his gaze lighted on the rack bearing the magi's coats of arms and his frantic confusion was swept away by a cold determination. He reached out for the nearest banner, on which long-limbed violet dragons cavorted across a sable field.

Leaning on the rail above, the bearded man smiled guardedly. 'A good choice, lad. That's Magus Byl's pennant. You'll find him a generous patron—if he deems you worthy to serve him, that is.'

'I'm not interested in his generosity,' said Altor, speaking quickly before he had time for second thoughts. 'Not for gold, at any rate.

I'll only ask him for one boon—'

The bearded man held up his hand. 'That's between you and him now. Go to meet him at the Blue Tower next to the Delicti Canal. Wait by the gargoyle trough.'

Carrying the pennant, Altor made his way off through the teeming streets. It was now getting dark and link-men scurried to and fro carrying flaring resin torches to light the way for shoppers and merrymakers.

A crier passed, extolling the virtues of his patron in a piercing nasal voice. Altor accosted him and got directions to the Delicti Canal. Turning off the main street, he left the noise and bustle behind and walked down a hushed alley. The sounds of festivity gradually faded into the distance. The canal was a ribbon of black ooze in the moonlight. Passing over a narrow bridge, Altor approached the darkened spire of a tower. A stone trough carved with gargoyle faces stood beside the door. Evidently this was where he was to wait.

A breeze blew along the canal and stirred a pungent odour up from the stone trough. It took Altor a couple of seconds to place the smell. He knew it from the funeral rites sometimes held at Osterlin Abbey. Charred bones.

Raking through the bed of damp ash filling the trough, he found a few hard fragments of bone. It was the remains of some kind of burnt offering. Then his fingers touched something else, and even as he brushed it clean for a closer look he began to feel a sense of mounting horror.

The object was a melted silver ring. This was the scene of a human sacrifice!

The moon glimmered behind dark clouds. The breeze stirred silver-sketched ripples on the black surface of the canal. Far off in the busy streets, the echoes of revelry sounded like the sighing of mournful ghosts. The tower seemed to radiant watchful silence.

Altor felt the hairs on his neck rise. Slowly he moved one hand to the hilt of his sword.

There was a rustling in the bushes behind the tower. Suddenly a black shape came somersaulting noiselessly through the air. It moved so silently that it might almost have been a trick of the light, but Altor's instincts were not fooled. He lashed out with the banner in his left hand and the figure jackknifed, plunging into the canal with a single heavy plop like a large stone.

Two more black-clad figures came from the direction of the bridge. Digging his hand into the trough, Altor flung bone-dust in their faces. They paused spluttering. Altor's sword shot from its scabbard, sliced the air. One head bounced across the cobblestones. The other assassin gave a muffled snarl and fell back clutching a gaping wound in his chest.

Something hissed through the air behind him. Altor whirled, snatching the banner around to use as a shield. The wooden haft splintered under the impact of two sharp-pronged throwing stars. Altor locked eyes with the one who had thrown them—a fourth man dressed all in black. This one also wore an amulet at his neck: a black badge decorated with prancing violet dragons.

He was reaching to his belt for another throwing star. Altor vaulted the trough, ducked low as the star went singing overhead, and came upright with his sword against the assassin's chest.

'That's Magus Byl's badge you wear,' said Altor. 'Why would he send you to kill his own champion? Talk!'

The assassin's only answer was a soft chuckle as though at a private joke. Slowly he lifted his head until he was staring Altor straight in the eye. Suddenly he swayed back. Altor, thinking he was trying to escape, pressed the sword-tip forward. But instead of dodging to one side, the assassin only gave a resigned shrug and thrust his body onto the blade. Blood spurted darkly in the moonlight. Giving a single gasp, the assassin convulsed and died.

Altor lowered the body to the cobblestones and wiped his sword clean. He did not resheathe it. Common sense told him that it would be best to give up any hope of working for Magus Byl. But both curiosity and the warrior's spirit drew him to the tower. It rose like a black talon against the star-dusted sky. Beyond its lightless windows, Altor was sure, lay the answer to the mystery. Why should the magus who sought to employ him have ordered his death? What had Magus Byl to gain?

He sighed and flung the door of the tower open. Enough moonlight spilled in to show a bare vestibule with a spiral stairway winding up towards the battlements. Ascending with sword in hand, Altor soon found himself in almost total darkness. Feeling his way a step at a time, he came to a doorway. He reached out to test it and it creaked open at his touch, admitting him to a moon-bathed sanctum.

The room seemed to be a shrine to one of the countless demon gods of Krarth. In the centre was a block of obsidian with a gore-soaked fur pelt draped across it—an obscene travesty of a holy altar. Pallid flames swam above iron basins on either side. A pall of grey vapour hung in the air at chest height. Beyond the altar, a wrought-iron gate led off into another chamber. Warily Altor crossed the room. Beyond the gate, the flickering flames barely illuminated a tall robed figure with skin like alabaster, stretched out across a black divan.

At the sound of Altor's approach, the figure stirred and looked up. At his mouth, sharp slivers of ivory caught the wan light. 'Well,' he said, his voice like the grating of a sarcophagus lid, 'I take it the mortal is dead.'

Altor ducked his head in a deep bow. 'Master, he is. Shall we... um..?'

'Drain off the blood, bring it to me. Burn the bones and meat as usual.'

Magus Byl scrutinized Altor for a moment in the gloom, then turned away and sank back on the divan. A jewelled cup rested on a table by his side, and from this he took a sip of something thick and dark.

Altor's heart was pounding. His instinct was simply to turn and flee, but he knew that he must do nothing to arouse the vampire's suspicions. 'And the pennant, master?' he said with a husky voice.

'Shall I return it to the recruiting booth?'

Magus Byl looked up sharply. Instantly he had uncoiled, so that now he no longer reclined languorously on the divan but stood upright. His black and purple robes cascaded like streams of frozen liquid over tarnished silver chainmail.

He extended a pale long-taloned hand. 'Come closer.'

Altor gritted his teeth. What had he said that had given him away? The assassins must have already had some arrangement for returning the banner and enticing more victims here. With his hands behind his back still holding the sword, he stepped closer.

A cruel sneer playing on his lips, Byl studied him through the iron gate. 'Thou art not my creature...'

'Nor shall I ever be!' cried Altor. Lunging with all his strength, he drove the sword between the bars of the gate. There was the scrape of steel on ancient marble-hard bone, a puff of dry brown dust as it impaled the vampire's heart, a deep grave groan from bloodless lips.

But, although crippled, Magus Byl did not fall. He raised his white hands to grip the gate. Altor, horror-struck, tugged at the sword but the hilt slipped out of his grasp. He backed away unarmed.

With the sword driven right through him, Byl resembled a giant insect impaled on a pin as he agonizingly inched the gate open. His voice escaped in gruesome gusts: 'Come, whelp... take back thy sword... Draw it from the stone of my heart, the cage of my bones... Now it is I who shall impale thee and drink deep of thy vein-wine...'

Altor, retreating, stumbled against the altar. Reaching out to steady himself, his hand squelched against the blood-soaked altar cloth.

The shock was all he needed to break the vampire's spell. Turning, he ran from the tower and did not stop until he stumbled back on the busy streets where merrymakers laughed and sang and the music banished thoughts of the stalking dead.

Three:

Caelestis

Altor returned to the main square, at this hour almost deserted except for a few beggars and stragglers on their way home. A torn scrap of paper fluttered past and he trod on it: a poster proclaiming the magi's contest.

The bearded steward was snoozing on a bench just inside his booth. Beside him, a brazier gleamed hot and red in the icy night air. As Altor approached he opened one eye and yawned, then blinked in puzzlement and sat forward to give the young warrior a closer look.

'Weren't you here earlier? You took Magus Byl's pennant.'

'Magus Byl apparently wasn't interested in the contest,' said Altor. He glanced at the rack, where one pennant still remained. 'Whose banner is that?'

'Magus Balhazar's.'

'And is he a vampire?'

The man chose to take this as a joke. 'I hardly think so!'

'Good.'

Altor reached for the banner, but just then there came a loud outcry from the far side of the square. He looked up to see the young dandy he had encountered earlier. His cloak swept out behind him like a bat's wings as he ran, and hot on his heels were several guardsmen of the night watch.

'Stop that thief!' bawled the irate sergeant of the guards as the young man came racing past the booth.

Altor stepped forward without thinking and put out one arm. The dandy skidded to a halt in front of him and glanced up in surprise.

For an instant their eyes locked, and Altor saw a look not of panic but of agile cunning. Then the young man ducked under his outstretched arm and reached for the last pennant. Altor lunged for it too. They both gripped the shaft at the same time.

The guardsmen pounded to a halt and began to fan out. 'So, villain,' gasped the sergeant, 'will you come quietly?'

The dandy looked at him in disdain. 'Villain, you say? I am Caelestis, the champion of Magus... of Magus...'

He turned to Altor who, although bewildered by the turn of events, found himself saying, 'Magus Balhazar.'

'Champion?' The sergeant tucked his thumbs in his belt and rocked with breathless laughter. 'You're no champion, lad. You're just a pickpocket and I'm taking you in.'

Caelestis stared back at him defiantly. The other guards hefted their cudgels and stood glowering. For a moment there was a tense silence, then the steward cleared his throat. 'The youngster's right,' he said. 'You can't arrest him now he's taken Magus Balhazar's banner.'

Altor suddenly realized what was happening. Tugging the banner away from Caelestis, he said, 'I was here first. Rightfully it is I who should be Magus Balhazar's champion.'

'Aha!' cried the sergeant in triumph. 'As I thought. Arrest this miscreant.'

Two of the guardsmen stepped closer. Caelestis wove away from them and snatched back the banner. 'Not so fast. The banner is mine. How can this oaf be the magus' champion? He doesn't even have a weapon.'

It was true. Altor had left his sword buried in Magus Byl's black heart. Rather than go into that now, he simply planted himself in a solid stance with his big arms folded across his chest. 'I need no weapons,' he protested. 'The monks of my order are trained to fight with empty hands if need be.'

'Indeed?' Caelestis cocked an eyebrow. 'I doubt whether Magus Balhazar would be impressed, however.'

Altor snorted in derision. 'Do you think he'll be impressed by having a pickpocket as his champion?'

The sergeant flung up his arms in exasperation. 'Enough!' He turned to the steward. 'What is the law? Are both these youths now employed by Magus Balhazar? Frankly I'd be happy to arrest the pair of them.'

'I have committed no crime!' pointed out Altor.

'And I myself am merely a suspect,' said Caelestis, 'until my case comes to trial.'

The steward leaned on the rail in front of his booth and stroked his beard thoughtfully. 'Both took the banner at the same time,' he announced at last, 'so both are eligible to serve the magus. Consequently they are immune from prosecution.'

At this the guards gave sighs of disappointment and started to wander off. The sergeant spat on the ground to show his opinion of the steward's judgement. Fixing Caelestis with a beady stare, he said, 'Just you wait, lad. I'll be waiting outside the Battlepits for you, and if you fail then you won't be able to count on the magus' protection.'

'If he fails,' said the steward laconically, 'then he'll be past caring about the laws of mortal men.'

Altor and Caelestis arrived at Magus Balhazar's mansion just as the gongs of the citadel were sounding the hour of midnight. A long avenue flanked by trees strung with paper lanterns ran from the gate to the white marble portico of the main entrance. The two youths stood outside in the street and watched a stream of elegantly costumed guests arriving in carriages. From inside the house wafted the strains of pipe music.

'It seems the magus is having a party,' remarked Caelestis. 'One of us is dressed for the occasion, at least.'

Altor had been struggling to keep his temper in check ever since the incident in front of the recruiting booth. Now he rounded on Caelestis and, grabbing him by the brocaded lapels of his jerkin, lifted him up onto his toes. 'Let's get something straight,' he growled.

'I've got no intention of teaming up with you for this contest. I need to win because I need a magical favour, and my best chance of winning will be on my own. When we meet Balhazar, I'm going to tell him that you only took the banner in order to avoid arrest for petty crime—'

Caelestis extricated himself from Altor's grip and smoothed down his lapels like a cat grooming itself after a scuffle. 'Surely I am innocent until proven guilty?' he objected. 'Unfortunately that sergeant was the sort of man to jump to conclusions, so if I'm to avoid jail it looks as if I must serve as Balhazar's champion. Believe me, if there was any alternative I'd take it. Unlike you, I'm hardly eager to risk life and limb in the Battlepits.'

'Fine,' said Altor. 'So leave now.'

'I'd be under arrest before dawn. No, my friend, I'm afraid we're in this together.'

Altor scowled. 'Come on, then. Just don't call me your friend.'

Sentries with drawn swords patrolled the avenue, icy-eyed men with grim faces of granite. They took no notice of the other party guests, but stared long and hard at Altor and Caelestis. As the two youths stepped through the gate, four of the sentries raised their swords and approached with a determined stride.

'Here's trouble,' Caelestis remarked out of the corner of his mouth.

But just as the sentries were about to challenge them, Altor raised the magus' banner. Its pattern of gold-&-scarlet eyes flared like fire in the light of the lanterns. The sentries saw it, and although their expressions remained as unchanging as if hewn from rock, the eager bellicosity in their eyes dulled to a look of disappointment. Grudgingly they waved Altor and Caelestis by.

At the door they were met by Balhazar's usher, a thin man with a bald pate and ginger sideburns that sprung in alarming tufts from the side of his face. 'Greetings!' he cried. 'Your names are not on the guest list, but the banner you bear is as good as any invitation.'

Caelestis looked past the usher into a spacious domed hall where the party was in full swing. All the revellers wore masks to conceal their identities. Pipers on a minstrel gallery overlooking the room played tunes to set the feet tapping, while on a dais behind the tables which almost overflowed with food and wine a group of lithe acrobats were performing a complex and spectacular dance.

A fetching girl in a costume of gauze and blue feathers caught Caelestis's eye. 'I think I'll mingle,' he said.

Altor planted the banner in front of him. 'We're not here for merriment,' he said to the usher. 'Will you take us to Magus Balhazar, please.'

Instead of answering at once, the usher summoned a footman with a brisk snap of his fingers. Pointing to the drinks and sweetmeats on the footman's tray, he said, 'My master will perhaps speak to you presently. In the meantime: eat and drink, enjoy yourselves.'

'I would enjoy myself more if I could see the magus right away,' insisted Altor. 'Since we are supposed to enter the Battlepits on his behalf tomorrow, partying is the last thing on my mind at the moment.'

'Oh, I don't know,' said Caelestis, tasting a jellied fruit from the tray. 'All work and no play, as they say...'

'There is nothing to prevent you from speaking to Magus Balhazar,' said the usher, 'if only you can identify him.'

Altor and Caelestis looked at him, but their puzzlement only provoked a broad grin which caused the ginger sideburns to rise like porcupine quills. With a theatrical flourish, the usher gestured behind him at the dozens of masked revellers.

'What do you mean?' asked Altor.

But Caelestis understood. 'It's a test. If we want to be Balhazar's champions we have to prove our worthiness.'

Altor stared around at the sea of masked faces. 'What sort of test is this?' he demanded. 'The Battlepits contest is a life-or death struggle, not a footling parlour game. Let me fight one of the magus's sentries if he wants proof of my skill.'

The usher only shook his head. 'My master wants a champion who is capable of more than just brute force. This test will show whether you have your wits about you.'

Altor and Caelestis exchanged a look, then slowly surveyed the room. It was a daunting prospect. How to identify the magus among all these revellers?

On the basis of costume, perhaps? There was a man in a sequined mask and jester's motley capering for the amusement of his friends... Too undignified. On a chaise-longue sat a well groomed gentleman in a domino cape romancing a girl in black velvet. But surely such familiarity would be unbecoming in a magus. Perhaps the man in the bear costume who stood at the back of the room swinging a bell without a clapper? No, too obscure—frivolous, even.

Caelestis glanced out into the garden. There two men stood beside a fountain, deep in conversation. One was dressed like a torturer, the other like a perfumed dandy.

Caelestis signalled to Altor. 'Possibly one of those is our magus,' he said, pointing the men out.

Altor grunted sceptically. 'Why not the fellow there in the green wig?'

Caelestis glanced across the room. 'He is talking to a servant. A magus would never do that.'

'How about the gaunt individual standing by the table? The one with the grey robe and blue face-paint.'

'Magus Uru's colours!' scoffed Caelestis. 'It's well known that Balhazar detests him.'

'That one there, then,' said Altor less certainly.

'I overheard him speak as we passed. He told a indelicate joke to two ladies, which is not the sort of conduct I'd expect of Magus Balhazar.'

'How would you know? Are you in the habit of attending his parties?'

'Well...' Caelestis appraised the man in question more carefully. 'Ah, see—he drinks pink claret from a long-stemmed glass! Do you suppose Magus Balhazar was raised in a pig sty, that he would behave with so little etiquette?'

Altor shook his head. 'Absurd. I think you're making all this up.

What possible reason do you have for thinking that Balhazar is one of those two by the fountain rather than any one of fifty others?'

Caelestis held up a finger. 'Well, let us see...' Cupping his hand to his mouth, he leaned over the balustrade of the patio.

'Balhazar!' came a plaintive voice from the fountain. 'Balhazar, hear me. I am a water sprite and I hereby serve notice that I have taken residence in your fountain. Please be so good as to have these fishes removed, as I find their company offensive.'

The man in the torturer's costume rounded on the fountain. 'What?' he cried, incensed. 'I will not be spoken to with such audacity! Get you gone at once from my fountain, sprite, or I'll shrivel you with spells of drought, desiccation and pollution!'

Caelestis vaulted over the balustrade, landed lightly on the grass beside the man, and bowed with a flourish of his feathered hat. 'My lord Balhazar, I presume.'

Balhazar stared at him, cheeks puffed with outrage. 'Who are you? How did you get in here? Is this your water sprite?'

'There is no water sprite,' said Caelestis with a wink. Cupping his hand, he threw his voice again, so that now it seemed as if Balhazar's wine-cup emitted a mirthful chuckle.

Altor, seeing that Balhazar was not finding these tricks as amusing as Caelestis did, quickly stepped in. 'Lord Balhazar, we've come to champion you in the Battlepits,' he announced, holding out the banner.

Balhazar glared from one to the other, eyes wide and white in a face purple with indignation. His mouth twisted to and fro. He seemed on the point of unleashing a curse that would fry them in their boots, then suddenly he threw back his head and gave a bellow of delighted laughter. 'Ah, what a jape! I thought my little test would root out a resourceful wizard to serve me. Instead, it seems, I've got myself a cunning knave and a crop headed monk!'

He waved his hand and instantly the party fell silent. Turning to face him, the hundreds of revellers bowed like marionettes and then dissolved into empty air.

'Illusions...' gasped Altor.

Without deigning to answer, Balhazar led the way in from the garden. They stood in an empty ballroom. The guests, the food the sentries and the dancing maidens—all were gone. Only the usher with the ginger sideburns remained.

'These are my champions,' announced Balhazar simply.

He had not paused to speak, but walked on past the usher and swept from the room. The usher turned to Altor and Caelestis with a smirk. 'Come, I'll show you to your rooms. Make yourselves comfortable by all means. The odds are that this is the last night of your lives.'

Four:

The Underworld

The usher came to fetch them when it was still an hour before dawn. 'The magus wishes to make an early start to avoid the crowds,' he said.

Altor had already been up for over an hour. The discipline of the monastery was in his bones, and after morning prayers and meditation had come the exercises that honed his battle skills and kept his body strong and supple.

Caelestis adhered to a very different regimen. Clutching the bedsheets, he snarled in protest as the usher tipped him out onto the floor.

'Getting cold feet?' said Altor. 'There's still a jail cell with your name on it.'

Caelestis grumbled and rubbed sleep out of his eyes. 'Cold feet, pah! We're only Balhazar's champions because I had the wit to pass his test. Where would you be if not for me? Still wandering around Magus Balhazar's ballroom gawping at illusory guests, that's where!'

The usher returned a few minutes later to escort them downstairs.

'For breakfast,' said Caelestis as they descended the stairs, 'I shall have three boiled plover's eggs, devilled kidneys, fried wild mushrooms, spiced sausage and some of those herb and turnip rissoles for which Krarthian cuisine is so justly renowned. No, on second thoughts make that two eggs—I don't want to be running around the Battlepits on an overfull stomach.'

A servant came over and held out a couple of pieces of toast on a plate. Altor grabbed his and gnawed on it while he went to look out of the door. Caelestis scowled and was about to wave the man away when hunger got the better of pride. He took the toast with a sigh.

Balhazar waited outside in the frosty courtyard with a retinue of foppish courtiers and rouged madams. Without a word to his champions, he climbed into a sedan chair and was borne aloft by four footmen in long blue leather coats. The retinue slowly filed out of the courtyard, following Balhazar's sedan chair along the grey pre-dawn streets.

'Quite a crowd,' remarked Altor, nodding to the townsfolk standing in sullen silence at the roadside.

Soldiers in the livery of the city militia came marching with raised pikes from a side street. The townsfolk made a show of cheering Balhazar's procession, only to lapse back into silence when the soldiers had gone.

'Apparently they're not enthusiastic about the magi's rule,' said Caelestis to one of the courtiers walking beside him.

The courtier shrugged. 'A ruler can either be loved or feared, never both.'

As they approached the city gate the crowds grew thicker. The retinues of other magi were also here. Altor saw a curtained carriage. The crest on its side, depicting a group of sinuous violet dragons on a black field, was familiar—as were the sable uniforms of the three champions walking beside it.

Caelestis noticed the look Altor gave the carriage as it went by. 'Who's that?' he asked.

'Magus Byl,' said Altor. 'I sought employment with him last night, but he already had his champions and was only interested in my blood. I thought I had killed him, but apparently I lost my old sword for nothing.'

'He wanted your blood? You mean he's a vampire?'

'I shouldn't speak ill of the dead. Let's just say he's not the type to go sunbathing.'

Caelestis whistled between his teeth. 'And let's hope he's not the type to bear a grudge, otherwise we can expect his three champions to come looking for us.'

'What difference does it make?' said Altor, shrugging. 'In this contest we're up against everyone else anyway.'

The procession left the city and headed out across the cold tundra. Groups of peasants already at work in the frost-hardened fields looked up glumly as the procession went past.

Along the horizon stretched a line of stone mounds, each an entrance to the underground catacombs where the contest would take place. The retinues of each of the magi made their way to one of the mounds. Not far off were three bronze-armoured barbarians, brothers from the Gnawing Wastes, who were championing Magus Tor. Altor watched them limbering up. They swung their huge battleaxes lustily and bellowed out huge gusts of steam into the chill air. Altor soon had their measure—they relied on energy rather than skill. An opponent who remained unintimidated by their shouts could soon beat them.

Satisfied, he turned his attention to the other champions he could see. Magus Kalugen, overlord of the city, had chosen an albino swordsman who had apparently won the contest for him last year, but had squandered his reward in a matter of months and now was forced to stake his life a second time. Altor saw the telltale signs of a year wasted on merrymaking: bleary eyes, swollen red nose, a slight paunch. The former champion already looked a beaten man.

Altor felt cold eyes on him. At one of the further mounds stood a solitary warlock whose name had been mentioned by one of the sentries: Icon the Ungodly, from Yamato in the distant east. He bore the pennant of Magus Uru. His twin swords were unscabbarded, the naked steel stamped with subtle runes.

Altor and Caelestis followed the carriage of Magus Balhazar to a heap of ancient stones where the magus' glyph was just visible on the heavy lintel, worn smooth by wind and snow and stained with brown lichen. Beneath it yawned an open pit that seemed to descend into the cold heart of the world.

The magi waited until all their champions were ready. There was silence apart from the wind howling across the plain. Each man looked around. For many it would be the last time they tasted fresh air or saw the daylight.

Altor stared down the dark tunnel. 'Curious to think that Death waits below for most of these men,' he muttered.

'Oh, very cheerful,' said Caelestis. 'That's the sort of pep talk your abbot would give you, eh? How about concentrating instead on the fabulous wealth that could be ours?'

Magus Kalugen raised his arms. All eyes turned to him. A portly man in white robes decorated with cursive slashes of black, he was transformed by the grandeur of the moment into an awesome figure. His voice, magnified by magic, boomed across the plain.

'Loyal and brave champions,' he said, 'you stand on the brink of the greatest adventure of your lives. Somewhere in the catacombs below our feet lies the Emblem of Victory. If you can find it and return it to the magus who has employed you, your reward will exceed the bounds of avarice. Other than this, the contest has no rules. Alliances and betrayals, stratagems and lies, duels and ambushes—all are fair game. Whether you live or die is written in the stars. So go down now and face your destiny.'

Kalugen lowered his arms. The wind returned, keening across the barren landscape, flattening the dry grass and whipping at cloaks and hair.

Altor and Caelestis looked at Magus Balhazar where he sat in his carriage. In a gesture of urbane disinterest, he extended his hand towards the entrance to the underworld. Then he turned away and signalled to his coachman to take him back to the city.

'I don't think he rates our chances,' said Caelestis.

Altor spat. 'Who cares? I'm not doing this for him. Are you ready?'

Other champions were already descending into their respective mounds. Altor led the way under the lichen-stained lintel and down stone steps into the darkness of the underworld.

Five:

The Gift Giver

They entered a chamber lit by torches flickering in brackets around the walls. Other than an alcove lined with sparkling mosaic, the rest of the room was of drab grime-encrusted stone. At the far end, a tunnel stretched off into the gloom.

Caelestis took one of the torches and handed another to Altor. 'We might need these. Balhazar didn't say whether the catacombs are illuminated throughout.'

Altor shook his head. 'You carry one if you like, but I'm a warrior. I prefer to keep my hands free for fighting.'

Caelestis shrugged. As Altor moved off towards the tunnel, he pointed to the alcove. 'Don't you think we ought to take a look at this first?'

'What for? There's nothing in it.'

'Take a look around you. Notice anything in particular?'

'It's just a plain stone chamber.'

'Precisely,' said Caelestis, nodding. 'Cold, dark, dingy—not out of place in your average dungeon. So why is that alcove decorated with blue and gold mosaics that obviously cost a small fortune? A clue, perhaps? A secret door?'

Altor gave an impatient sigh. 'Go on, then, take a look. But make it quick.'

Caelestis stepped over and examined the alcove by the light of his torch. It looked as if it was supposed to hold a vase or life-size statue, but there was nothing in it now. The mosaics were cut into delicate interlocking shapes and threw back spangles of colour from the flames. Deftly Caelestis ran his fingers around the edge, feeling for a hidden catch...

'Hurry up,' said Altor.

'All right!' Caelestis snapped back. Abandoning caution, he climbed up into the alcove.

There was a blinding flash of light. The floor fell away from under him as though it had suddenly turned to liquid. The glittering mosaic spun in front of his eyes, painting blurred colours of blue and gold.

After an instant of dizziness the ground steadied. He took a deep breath and was surprised to find himself tasting clean air and not the musty atmosphere of the Battlepits. As his vision cleared, he saw he was now in a garden under a high roof of coloured glass that filtered the light into rainbow shards. In front of him was a bubbling fountain, and perched on the edge of this was an elfin girl clad in a swathe of green silk.

Caelestis opened his mouth to speak, but for once his silver tongue was tied. 'Who..? What..? Where..?' he said, then realized that for the sake of his dignity he would do better to keep quiet.

'I am Larisha,' said the elf in a voice of honey and fine fragrances. 'By the ancients of Krarth I was called the Gift Giver. Now that you have stumbled into my little bower, I am obliged to render you one gift.'

Caelestis had recovered his wits enough to make a courtly bow. 'Miss Larisha, I am charmed to make your acquaintance. Merely to look upon such beauty is a gift in itself.'

Larisha turned away, her hair falling across her face but not quite concealing a smile of pleasure at Caelestis' words. She reached into the waters of the fountain and held up a silver sword. 'This is the blade used by Vislet, the Prince of Asmuly, who once bested a hundred foes in the space of a single day.' She allowed it to fall back into the water and then pulled out another item. 'And this golden ring belonged to Shormiano the wizard, and this—' she dropped the ring and took a large gem from the water '—is the frozen last breath of Astarandel the Dragonlord.'

Caelestis noticed a flicker of light in the orange depths of the gem. Somehow, although faint, it seemed to suggest the roaring heart of an inferno. 'What does it do?' he asked. 'That and the other items?'

Larisha lifted her slender shoulders in a careless shrug. 'It is not for me to say. I am here merely to dispense one of these things as a gift.'

'Well, thank you...' said Caelestis, peering down into the waters of the fountain as he struggled to choose.

Larisha waved her hand dismissively. 'Do not trouble to thank me, for I am a creature without a soul, without free will. I merely perform the duty assigned to me by the Fates.'

A crafty look came into Caelestis's eye. 'Why, that is absurd,' he said quickly. 'How can you describe yourself as soulless, you who are more lovely than any earthly woman? Behold your exquisite reflection in this fountain. Can you possibly deny that it is the face of a vibrant elemental soul, a passionate beauty who laughs in the face of the cruel Fates!'

Larisha looked startled for a moment, then turned to regard herself in the crystal water of the fountain. A laugh bubbled up from inside her, and she tossed her head in delight like a proud mare. 'Why you speak truly,' she exclaimed, smiling into her reflection and becoming even more pleased by what she saw. 'Let us spite the Fates, then—those horrendous crones! I'll give you all three gifts, not because I must but because I freely choose to do so.'

Caelestis concealed his grin of triumph with a flourish of his sleeve as he bowed again. 'Then, since it is by your own will and not the dictates of destiny that I receive these gifts, I need show no restrain in thanking you.' So saying, he stepped forward and planted a kiss on the elf girl's brow.

Startled, Larisha stood up, trailing her silk toga like a green shadow, and thrust the three gifts towards him. Caelestis was disconcerted to find her several inches taller than himself. He had always imagined elves would be small creatures. Taking the sword and ring and gemstone, he stepped back.

'Return now to the magi's labyrinth,' said Larisha, lifting her hands to weave a spell. 'And you may take another gift with those three, if it is of use to you—the gift of my good wishes in your quest.'

Colours and sounds jangled and swirled. Caelestis was again jerked off his feet, then just as abruptly the ground solidified under him. He was back in the alcove.

Altor was staring at him open-mouthed. 'Where did you go?' he asked. 'And how, come to that?'

'It's a bit difficult to explain, seeing as how I've got no idea myself. But I met an elf that gave me these.'

Altor took the silver sword and first tested its edge on the hairs on the back of his hand, then swung it through the air with approval. Not only was it finely forged and razor-keen, but it was perfectly balanced for his hand.

'You keep that, then,' said Caelestis. He slipped the golden ring onto his finger. He had hoped for a sudden surge of power or at least an inkling of some magic it might contain, but to his chagrin there was nothing.

He looked up to find Altor regarding him suspiciously. 'What?'

'Did you steal these things, Caelestis?'

'Of course not. It's a magical place, this, isn't it? That's the sort of thing that happens around here. You get whisked off to mysterious gardens and meet elf maidens who give you things.'

'Oh, it was a female elf, was it?' said Altor.

'A good job you weren't the one to meet her,' said Caelestis scornfully. 'I don't think an apprentice monk like you would've known where to look! As it was, I gave her a compliment for the sword, a kiss for the ring, and a heartfelt thank-you for this gemstone. I consider it fair exchange, and therefore not thievery.'

'Well,' Altor admitted, 'I certainly needed a sword.'

'Pardon me?' Caelestis cupped a hand to his ear. 'Did I hear you correctly? It sounded almost as if you think I've done something right.'

Altor flung up his hands. 'Yes, yes, all right. You did well, Caelestis.

You were right about the alcove and I was wrong. Thanks for the sword, but now—don't you think we should be getting a move on?'

Caelestis gave him a broad smile. 'Lead on, my friend. I'm right behind you.'

They advanced into a red-tiled corridor whose walls were lined with gold-framed mirrors. The torchlight hovered in multiple dim halos to either side, reflected in the mirrors beneath a thick layer of dust. The sound of their footsteps on the cold tiles echoed obtrusively in the silence. Altor, in the lead, felt a sense of unease that grew with each step.

At last they reached the end of the corridor. Vast double doors of bronze stood ahead, stamped with ancient symbols from the days when Krarth had been ruled by the True Magi, the superhuman wizards who were the forerunners of Kalugen and his ilk.

Caelestis wiped a smear of dust from one of the mirrors and adjusted his hair in the winking torchlight. 'Which way now?' he mused.

'Have we got a choice?' said Altor, looking back over his shoulder. 'And haven't you got anything better to do than preen yourself like a cock partridge?'

'A man should always strive to be well turned-out,' replied Caelestis, unruffled. 'And since you ask, yes, we do have a choice. See the catch?' He pointed to the frame of the mirror. 'This mirror conceals a secret door.'

'I think we should—' Altor began to say.

But Caelestis had already prised open the catch. As he swung the mirror away from the wall, they saw that there was indeed a narrow passage beyond.

The weight of the heavy mirror tugged at hinges weakened by age. Slipping out of Caelestis' hand, it fell to the tiled floor and smashed into jagged fragments.

The noise reverberated along the corridor and, at this, an eager wailing rose in the air.

Caelestis looked around in alarm. 'Great God, listen to that!

Where's it coming from?'

Altor pointed to the other mirrors. The glass bulged outwards as though something was pushing its way out from behind. The wailing grew until it was a single sustained note—a tortured scream drawn out to the limit of hearing.

The mirrors burst outwards in a shower of broken glass. From the walls on either side reached hulking grey arms with ragged fingernails like shards of mica. But, unlike the mirror Caelestis had opened, behind these others there were no secret passages. By some sorcery the grey creatures had been trapped inside the glass itself.

'Watch out!' cried Caelestis.

Altor whirled and slashed at one, severing its wrist, and found himself staring into a face with hollow eye-sockets and a leering cyanide-blue slit for a mouth.

With horror he realized that the creature had once been a living man.

Six:

The Faltyn

Altor turned to shout a warning, but it was not needed. Caelestis was already diving into the passage behind the mirror he had opened. 'Come on!' he called back.

Altor paused briefly, not liking to run from a fight, but discretion soon got the better of his martial instincts. There were too many of the creatures for one man to fight, and in any case he wasn't sure his sword could kill things that were no longer truly alive. He squeezed along the passage behind Caelestis and was relieved to find that the cadaverous grey monsters were too big to follow.

The passage was rough-hewn and very weathered, as if tunnelled into the bedrock of the Keep aeons before the coming of mankind. After a while it widened a little, but they still had to crouch as they worked their way up a twisting flight of slippery rock-cut steps and then down a long pebble-strewn ramp.

At last they reached a small cave with a metal grille set into the floor. A pale shaft of light stabbed up from below. Peering through the grille, they saw a corridor of grey marble lit by oil lamps on ledges along the walls. Caelestis lay down full-length on the floor of the cave with his face pressed to the grille. By craning his neck he could see that the corridor ended in a bronze-bound portal.

'Can we prise it up?' said Altor, crouching to examine the grille.

'Ssh,' warned Caelestis. 'I can hear someone coming.'

There was the sound of a key being turned, loud and ominous in the empty corridor. The bronze door swung open with a screech of corroded hinges. Three burly barbarians strode forward, slamming the door behind them without concern for whether or not they were heard. Not thinking to look up, they stopped directly under the grille and took out a scrap of parchment.

'What's it say, Erek?' muttered one.

'I'm not sure, Snorri,' said the man with the parchment, idly plucking a flea out of his hair and crunching it in his teeth. 'I can't read, can I?'

'By Muninn and Huginn!' bellowed the third barbarian, a red bearded ox of a man. 'Have you no learning at all, Erek?' He snatched the parchment from his comrade and peered at it. 'Well, it says... it says... Damn this light, it's too dim to read by! Well, I reckon it says one of the passages ahead is a dead end. But what do you want to listen to a bit of ink and parchment for? The only way to find out is to see for ourselves...'

The three swaggered off down the corridor, loudly discussing the ale they would buy with their reward money after winning the contest.

Caelestis smiled wryly. 'A clear case of counting one's chickens...' he said when the barbarians had passed out of earshot.

'Did you get a good look at them?' said Altor. 'Were they Magus Tor's champions?'

'No, those were from the Gnawing Waste, weren't they? I think this lot must be Mercanian. And none too bright either.'

'You don't need to be all that bright to chop a man down with a sword.'

This provoked a gleeful grin from Caelestis. 'You said it, warrior, I didn't!'

Altor was not too pompous to laugh at himself. 'Okay, you do the thinking and I'll do the chopping, deal? Give me a hand with this grille.'

It pulled free easily and they were able to squeeze through. Caelestis dropped the torch to Altor before joining him in the marble corridor.

'We won't need this any more,' said Altor, nodding at the oil lamps.

Caelestis stroked his chin thoughtfully, but hung onto the torch.

'Maybe I'm being a pessimist, but I don't want to toss it away and then find we have to find our way across an unlit cavern.'

'Fine, since you're the one who's carrying it.' Altor led the way along the corridor until they reached a junction. One passage was paved with black marble, the other with white. Above the junction, a carving decorated the wall. It showed a man's head in outline, a profile view looking to the left. A series of lines radiated from the head like spokes from the hub of a wheel.

'It looks like the barbarians' map was accurate. Which way?'

'It's Sorrisday, so right is lucky.'

'Left, then,' Altor decided.

After a short distance the white-floored corridor ended in a heavy oak door studded with bosses of burnished copper. Caelestis was about to suggest they stopped to listen when Altor, hearing the clash of metal from the other side, wrenched it open.

They stepped through to a scene of carnage. Two of the barbarians lay writhing in their death-throes on the floor, glistening spikes protruding from livid wounds on their necks. The third was still on his feet although he too had a poison dart in his shoulder. Swaying as though drunk, he was struggling with two black-robed assassins wielding crescent-shaped swords. Just as Altor and Caelestis burst in, one of the assassins aimed a scything cut at the surviving barbarian's wrist. Hand and sword dropped to the floor, but instead of falling the huge barbarian roared and thrust the bleeding stump of his arm into the nearest assassin's face.

Altor crossed the room in two paces and impaled the other assassin on his sword. He withdrew the blade on the backswing, reversed it and drove it through the other assassin's neck from the side.

Seeing his foe go limp, the barbarian gave a deep groan and slumped to a sitting position on the floor. His severed arm continued to pump bright scarlet blood, and his face was now the colour of wet chalk.

'I'm done for,' he said thickly. 'Take our map. We got it off Magus Xon and it's been right this far.'

Caelestis paused to check that both assassins were dead and then crouched with Altor beside the rapidly weakening barbarian. 'Anyone you want us to take a message to?' he asked, adding: 'As long as it's convenient, of course—can't promise anything.'

'My wife's waiting up above,' gasped the barbarian. 'Tell her... tell her...'

The huge frame jerked and went limp, all the muscles suddenly like clay. Altor laid the body to the floor and closed its staring eyes.

'Guess we'll never know what to tell his wife,' said Caelestis.

'I do,' said Altor grimly. 'He wanted her to know he died in battle.'

'That's a pretty fair bet in a place like this, isn't it!' snorted Caelestis. 'I think she'd guess he didn't die of old age.'

Altor glared at him. 'Have you no respect for men of honour, Caelestis?'

'Sure. Respect, Olaf, or whatever his name was. But I'm not convinced by this palaver about 'glorious deaths'. I think it might be that some people prefer the idea of a quick death in battle to real life.'

'Pah, you understand nothing.'

'Whatever.' Caelestis shrugged. 'Mind telling me why you were so quick to chip in on the barbarian's side? I mean, considering that anyone we meet down here is potentially our deadly enemy.'

'You could say it was because I didn't like the odds,' said Altor. 'But the truth is I met some assassins like this last night. They work for Magus Byl, and I had a score to settle.'

They took stock of the room. Faced entirely in gleaming white marble, it reflected the light of the candelabra above with dazzling intensity.

Caelestis ran his fingers over the wall. 'No secret doors this time.'

With no other route available, they retraced their steps and took the black-paved corridor. It led to steps that descended into candlelit gloom. The sound of dripping water reached their ears from below.

Caelestis held up the torch. Droplets showed on the walls. 'I do hope I don't get my cloak wet,' he said. 'The damp can completely ruin velvet.'

Altor laughed scornfully. 'How inconsiderate of the magi not to see to little things like that!'

Descending for several minutes, they finally reached a brick archway leading through into another corridor which ended in a colossal doorway adorned with classical designs. Tall bronze candelabra lined the foyer in front of the door, flooding the underworld with pale gold light, but Caelestis and Altor hesitated. Between them and the door stood a motionless figure, leaning idly against the wall with his back turned. In the candlelight they could make out his jet-black ringmail armour and ochre tabard. Here and there rust spots showed like clots of dried blood through the links of his armour.

'Another of the champions?' Altor whispered.

Caelestis drew him back behind the brick arch. 'No, I recognize the uniform. He's a soldier of the Battalion of Torment—the militia of Kalugen's dungeons. Tomb rangers, some call them. They're recruited from condemned cells.'

'For what purpose?'

'To guard crypts and catacombs. To keep out grave robbers and the like.'

Altor gave Caelestis a shrewd look. 'I didn't think even you would stoop that low.'

'You can't take it with you, even if some of them try to,' Caelestis said with a casual shrug. 'All I do is make sure wasted currency gets back into circulation. Anyway, the point is these guys are hard nuts. They might spend months or even years without seeing the light of day, and they'll take on anyone.'

Altor lifted his sword. 'Me too.' He stepped out into the light.

The ranger looked up without surprise. He did not even bother to uncross his arms, let alone reach for the sword at his belt.

'I don't suppose you'll make this easy on yourself?' said Altor.

'What, and miss out on some fun?' answered the ranger with a sneer.

Caelestis moved out from behind the arch. 'Be careful, Altor.'

The ranger glanced at him lazily. 'Two of you, huh?'

'It will be a fair fight, by my honour,' said Altor quickly.

'Fair? But you have a magic sword... How about barehanded?'

The ranger unbuckled his sword and tossed it behind him. Only Caelestis noticed the crafty gleam that had appeared in his eyes. To his dismay, Altor responded to the taunt by sheathing the silver sword and placing it carefully against the wall. 'No, Altor,' he said urgently. 'He's up to something.'

Altor dropped into a fighting crouch as the ranger moved slowly towards him. Both had their arms raised, hands open like wrestlers waiting for an opening. But just as the ranger came within arm's reach, he threw himself past Altor in a somersault and snatched up the silver sword from where it was propped against the wall.

'Trickery,' said Altor in a disappointed voice, but he didn't waste any time berating the tomb ranger for not fighting fair. Instantly he dived to where the other sword lay.

The ranger just grinned. 'Yeah, go on—be my guest.'

Altor drew the sword. It was just the stump of a blade, snapped off inches from the hilt.

'Fair exchange?' taunted the ranger.

Caelestis knew he was no match for a tomb ranger himself. Drawing his own sword, he tossed it to his friend. 'Altor, catch!'

The tomb ranger whirled and exploded into action. The sword in his hands became a blurred silver arc and, with a clang, Caelestis's sword was struck from the air before Altor could catch it.

'That wouldn't be fair,' said the ranger with a snide grin. 'Can't have you substituting your weapon halfway through the fight.'

He moved forward, slicing to left and right. Altor barely dodged away from the lethal blade.

Caelestis watched helplessly. The tomb rangers lived only for violence and killing. Their motto was 'Death is my brother' and they acknowledged no other creed. Even in a fair fight the odds would be stacked against Altor—and this was far from a fair fight.

The ranger pretended to slash to Altor's head then, as the young warrior ducked, he changed the attack to a thrust which drew a red mark of blood across Altor's cheek. Caelestis clenched his hands. 'I wish I could get my sword—' he muttered. But the ranger was standing right over it.

'A simple enough request...' remarked a voice by his elbow.

Astonished, Caelestis looked round to see a thin elfish figure with powder-blue skin and lavender hair. 'Who—? What—?' He closed his mouth and waited for his brain to catch up with his tongue. 'What are you?'

The outlandish creature buffed its nails on its sleeve and slowly floated up into the air until it appeared to be reclining on an invisible divan. 'I am the Faltyn—the genie, if you will, of that ring you wear.'

'That is handy,' said Caelestis, adapting at once to the new situation. 'In a moment I will explain the jewels and other finery that I require. First, I wish you to attend to a pressing problem: turn that tomb ranger into a roast suckling pig.'

The Faltyn wagged a finger at him. 'I am no slave,' it replied. 'For each service I must be properly paid.'

The clash of metal rang out. Altor was parrying desperately with the broken sword in his hand, but the ranger had him backed into a corner. The silver sword flashed to and fro, a flicker of white fire in the candlelight. Red sparks and chips of rusty metal leapt from Altor's blade as he parried again. The ranger was clearly toying with him. Defeat—and death—were only moments away.

'Fine, fine,' said Caelestis to the Faltyn. 'I'll pay you. Just get me my sword.'

'I may choose my payment?'

'Yes!'

The Faltyn gave a broad contented smile. 'Then I choose the stone.'

Caelestis was puzzled for an instant, then he fished in his pocket and drew out the fiery orange gem that was one of the three gifts Larisha had given him. 'This?'

The Faltyn shook its head. 'No, the other one...'

At that moment Altor sensed the grim approach of death. The

ranger, tiring at last of this sadistic sport, easily knocked the broken stub of sword out of his hand. Crouching at bay, Altor waited defiantly for the fatal stroke.

'The Battlepits are no place for callow youths,' sneered the tomb ranger. 'Even seasoned veterans fear to venture down here. You should never have come.'

'Kill me by all means,' snarled Altor. 'Just don't pretend that skill had anything to do with it.'

'You think I cheated?' The ranger gave a growl that was half a laugh. 'This isn't about fair play, boy. You made a wager with Death when you entered here. Surely you realized you'd be playing with marked cards?'

Before Altor could reply, the ranger's expression changed from a sneer to a puzzled frown. They both looked down at the same time. Several inches of slender steel were protruding from the ranger's chest.

'We switched the deck,' said Caelestis from behind him as the ranger slumped to the floor.

'Nice moves...' gasped the ranger. 'I never heard you coming.' Then his eyes glazed over and he lay still.

Caelestis withdrew his blade and wiped it on the dead man's tunic. Altor retrieved the silver sword and gave a heartfelt sigh. 'Caelestis, I owe you an apology! Everything I said about you, I take it all back. You saved my life. You're okay in my book!'

'Will you still say that, I wonder,' called the Faltyn, 'when you see what he has given me?'

Altor looked up and saw the Faltyn for the first time, hovering directly above his head on a pillow of ethereal blue vapour.

'What on earth—?' he began, but then he saw the object the Faltyn was holding triumphantly between its fingers.

It was the pommel stone!

Seven:

Death's Boatman

'How did you get that?' shouted Altor. He grabbed for the stone, but the Faltyn drifted up out of reach.

'Your friend will tell you,' said the Faltyn. 'As for myself, I now return with my prize to the ring.'

The Faltyn gleamed bright blue, then faded rapidly like an afterimage on the back of the eye. Within seconds there was nothing to show it had ever existed, except for a faint flowery scent in the air—and the growing anger in Altor's heart.

He grabbed Caelestis by the neck. 'You gave it the pommel stone? Where... where, Caelestis..?' He gritted his teeth, too beside himself with rage to think clearly.

'Where did I get it? Ah, well... loosen your grip, Altor, it's a bit hard to, er, speak when your windpipe's being crushed.'

Altor let go and stood glaring at him. 'Go on, then. And make it good.'

'Yes...' Caelestis smoothed out his jerkin, thoughtfully adjusted the tilt of his hat. 'You know how it is, Altor, when you've never met someone. They're a stranger, right? You don't owe them anything, they don't owe you—'

'Our Lord taught that all men are brothers,' said Altor, making it sound like some kind of curse.

'Ah! And, yes... didn't He also preach that we should forgive others? The sinner that repents is worth two in hell, or something...'

Caelestis fell silent. Altor stood staring at him for a few seconds. His anger had gone; now he felt only bitter disappointment. 'You stole it, didn't you?' he said with icy calm. 'You picked my pocket and stole it. I can't believe that. How could you stoop so low?'

'I admit, er, I have no substantive defence in law. Um, I can only plead mitigating circumstances—namely, I was somewhat impoverished and much in need at the time. Which is why that other pickpocketing incident occurred later, for which the militia were trying to arrest me...'

'It wasn't an isolated case, then? That makes me feel much better!'

Caelestis spread his hands imploringly. 'What can I say? I didn't know that stone was the reason you got into the contest in the first place, did I? I'd have given it back if we get through all this in one piece.'

'Except now you've given it to a magic sprite!' cried Altor with a bitter laugh. 'There's nothing to discuss. You're a lowlife pickpocket, a sometime tomb robber, you stole from me, cheated your way into this contest to escape arrest...'

'I saved your life, though. And got you that sword.'

'We'll call it quits. When this is all over, assuming we survive, we'll go our own separate ways and not a moment too soon. Until then, Caelestis, try not to do anything else to annoy me.'

'Fine,' said Caelestis, equally peeved. 'I'll just let you get yourself killed next time, then, shall I?'

They stepped through the ornamental door into a vast cavern whose walls sparkled with veins of glowing quartz. Rock-cut steps led down to a pebble beach washed by the dark waters of an underground lake. A smooth slab of grey rock with a sculpted frieze running around it jutted into the lake to make a kind of jetty. There were no boats moored there.

'Can you swim?' asked Altor.

'If that's a general enquiry, then yes. If you're asking whether I'm prepared to swim across that—forget it!'

'What choice have we got?'

Caelestis looked around, then he pointed out four large blocks further along the beach. They looked like sarcophagi built on a monumental scale. 'Maybe we'll find something there.'

Descending the steps, the two trudged across the wet pebbles for a closer look. The sarcophagus lids depicted four goblin glowering ancients in regal attire. Each was more than twice the height of a man, and Caelestis shuddered when he thought what creatures might lie buried there.

'I thought a one-time tomb robber would be made of sterner stuff,' said Altor with a smile.

'The trick is to be selective about whose tomb you rob,' said Caelestis. 'Giant ancient wizards are a definite no-no.'

Altor reached thoughtfully towards the nearest sarcophagus, then paused. The lid was encrusted with the undisturbed mould of many years.

'Aren't you going to open it?' whispered Caelestis nervously. 'Not that I want to encourage you, mind.'

Altor shook his head. 'From what the ranger said, we can't be the first to reach this far. That means whoever's ahead of us found a way to cross the lake without opening these caskets.'

Caelestis nodded, not bothering to hide his relief. 'The jetty, then...'

They walked back to the jetty, a rounded slab of slippery wet stone like the shell of a giant whelk. Crouching down, Altor examined the frieze running around it. 'Maybe there's a clue here,' he mused.

Caelestis bent over and examined the carvings with pursed lips. 'Those are musical notes. It's just an old tune—The Gondolier or something. Surely you've heard it?'

He whistled a snatch of the refrain, then stopped. The notes wafted forlornly off into the darkness across the water.

The ripples came first, stirring the glistening black water against the sides of the jetty. Then the soft sigh of a single oar, and a boat hung with dark blue drapes slid into view as if congealing out of the void. As it drew nearer, a boatman became visible although somehow they had failed to notice him at first. He worked his oar with thin but apparently tireless arms, bringing the boat to a halt beside the jetty.

Waves lapped the shore, producing an eerie shush-shush like a great beast breathing deeply in its sleep.

Altor and Caelestis watched the boatman. His scrawny frame was wrapped in odd folds of cloth, his face hidden by one of the despondent theatrical masks used in Ancient Emphidian tragedies. He stood in silence as though waiting for something.

'You know what I said about not needing to open the sarcophagi?' ventured Altor.

Caelestis gave him a wary sidelong glance. 'Yes...'

'Well, I think we will have to after all.'

Caelestis sighed. 'Somehow I knew it. But why?'

'From what I remember of mythology, this must be the ferryman of the souls of the dead. The Ancient Emphidians called him Keron, which the peasants of modern Ellesland have corrupted to Stug the Careworn—'

'Spare me the history lesson, Altor.'

'Well, I think he needs payment before he'll ferry us across the lake. The ancients used to bury their dead with a coin under the corpse's tongue so that the soul would have something to pay him with.'

Caelestis looked back along the beach to where the four sarcophagi waited. When he tried to swallow, he found his mouth had gone as dry as parchment. 'Okay, let's do it,' he said grimly.

Sheathing his sword, Altor strode up to the nearest sarcophagus and placed his shoulder against the lid. He leant forward and braced his feet solidly in the wet shingle. For long moments he strained in silence. The whiteness of his face and the hard cords of muscle in his neck gave the only clues as to his titanic exertion. Then at last he gave a gasp that was echoed by the grating of stone, and the lid slid aside leaving a small gap.

Altor staggered back, leaning on his knees while he got his breath back. Caelestis peered dubiously into the dark slit between the lid and the side of the sarcophagus. A smell that reminded him of incense and dusty garments rose in the clammy air.

'Go on, then,' said Altor as he straightened up and drew his sword.

'Why me?' protested Caelestis.

'My hand wouldn't fit in that small a gap, for one thing.'

'And what else?'

'Well...' Altor grinned. 'If the corpse comes to life I'd better be ready to fight it.'

Caelestis glared at him. 'Thanks a lot. I'd managed to keep my mind off that possibility until now.'

Turning back to the sarcophagus, he held his hand over the gap as if he were steeling himself to plunge it into icy-cold water. Then, with a deep breath, he reached inside.

His fingers felt a hard bony dome covered with a few dry wisps of hair. The skin crackled away under his touch like old tissue paper. Choking with disgust, he felt down across the sharp nub of bone that marked the corpse's nose, over dry crumbling lips... His fingers probed between the teeth.

'Argh!' he screamed suddenly. 'It's got me. Help, Altor! It's biting my hand off!'

Altor was so shocked that he bounded forward, lost his footing on the shingle, and sat down hard. Caelestis stopped screaming and dissolved instead into fits of giggles. 'I had you going there, didn't I?' he laughed, drawing his hand out of the sarcophagus to show the antique silver coin he'd found.

'You toad,' said Altor, picking himself up. 'I really thought it had got you.'

'Ah, come on. It was just a joke. It was you that put the idea into my head, after all.'

Altor managed a rueful smile. 'I guess I deserved it. Let's see if the boatman will accept our payment.'

They returned to the jetty and now the boatman spoke from the first time behind his mournful mask. 'The fee is one obol.'

'How about this?' said Caelestis, putting the silver coin into the boatman's clay-pale hand.

'It will suffice. Come aboard.'

He waited until they had settled themselves on the bench under the boat's blue awning, then pushed off from the jetty. Eddies of water swirled beneath them, as dark and impenetrable as the depths of the night sky. Above, the roof of the cavern swept up to vast heights where stalactites hung like the chandeliers of a great cathedral. Staring ahead into the gloom, they could not make out the far shore of the lake, and since by now they had lost sight of the jetty as well it was as though they were drifting in an immense void.

A buoy loomed out of the darkness. Its wood had been chewed away by countless tides, its iron fretwork reduced to clots of dark red rust. Two lines of writing were carved into the rotted wood.

'Stop here,' said Caelestis to the boatman.

Altor looked at him quizzically.

Caelestis leaned over to study the writing, then shook his head. 'I thought it might be a warning of what's ahead, but I can't read it.'

There was a heavy iron chain attached through a link to the side of the buoy. It trailed down into the deeps. 'What do you think that is?' said Altor.

'It's obvious. You pull on it and it drains the lake.' Caelestis watched the puzzled look spread over Altor's face before cracking a smile. 'No, I don't know. Treasure, maybe?'

Neither of them noticed that the boatman had grown suddenly nervous. His lean fingers twitched as he gripped the oar, but he said nothing.

Altor came to a decision. 'We can't afford to ignore it; it might be something we need. Give me a hand to pull it up.'

They hauled on the chain. At first it refused to budge, but then with a slow sucking of lake-bed mud it began to give. Altor pulled up hand after hand of dripping rust-caked links, and at last the object on the other end came into view. It was a metal gibbet cage containing a mire-coated skeleton.

An emerald talisman winked in the dim light. Caelestis reached for it, only to jump back like a startled cat as the skull's eye sockets gave a blaze of green light.

Quickly Altor let go of the chain. As the grisly catch slipped back into the depths, plumes of green vapour rose from the bones. Bubbling and seething noxiously above the water, they began to weave together, coalescing into a monstrous diffuse shape...

Altor and Caelestis drew back aghast as a luminous phantom formed with clutching talons and eyes like beacons.

'Free!' it howled in a hollow voice. A ghastly rictus spread across its face. 'Now you who have freed me must take my place.'

Altor cut with his sword as the phantom reached towards them. The blade passed through its fingers with no more effect than it would have had on smoke. But the two comrades could feel the deathly energy of the phantom's claws like waves of icy air in their face. It might not be solid, but they were in no doubt that it could kill them all the same.

Missing Altor by inches, the phantom's fingers clawed into the awning. There was a sound like the sky tearing and the awning ripped apart into billows of royal blue. Realising its mistake the creature gave a howl of outrage and a bolt of icy green flame emanated from its grinning maw. The awning caught alight like dry paper. Caelestis sprang up and pulled the rest of the awning off its frame, dodging the leaping flames and wobbling precariously as the boat rocked.

Altor, sprawled on the floor of the boat, fumbled for his sword. As Caelestis flung the blazing fabric overboard into the black water the cave went momentarily dark, allowing Altor to see a bright glow emanating from his sword. Snatching it up, he rose in a low balanced posture and in one smooth movement swung again at the phantom.

The sword sliced through empty air as before, but this time Altor thought he felt a slight tug, as if the blade had in fact caught on something as it passed through the creature. The phantom's eerie green glow flickered for a moment like a guttering torch.

' Swim for it!' yelled Caelestis. 'We can't fight this thing!'

Altor was preparing for another swing. 'Not yet!' he called. 'The sword can hurt it.'

The boat rocked crazily again, throwing Altor off balance, and there was a splash in the water behind them.

Caelestis looked behind him. The sinister boatman had gone. Some distance away something was moving rapidly away, not swimming but gliding along just below the surface of the water like an eel. So even the mythical boatman Keron didn't care to confront this shrieking phantom. Caelestis needed no convincing. His instinct for self preservation, honed in the backstreets of a dozen teeming cities, told him it was time to get out. He turned to call to Altor again.

Then he heard the scrape of claws along the planks of the boat. The phantom, plunging its claws into the water, was trying to crack open the hull like a nut.

Altor was getting to his feet again when he was snatched from behind by Caelestis, who launched them both into the water. Just in time—an instant later the phantom's hand came stabbing through the planks and the boat split like kindling. Caelestis heard its hollow roar of rage at missing its prey, then the water enveloped him in throbbing silence.

Altor got a lungful of lake water and flailed in panic for a few seconds. As he got a grip on himself, he turned towards the dim light above and kicked up towards the surface. He seemed to rise slowly as though engulfed in a tar pit, but at last his head broke the surface. He gagged and spat out the murky water which tasted of chill decay. It was so horrible that for a few moments he could do nothing but tread water, spluttering to clear his mouth of the vile taste.

Not far off the phantom was demolishing the boat in silence, the only sounds the snapping and crunching of wood. Slowly, as Altor watched, it dispersed into wisps of green mist that hung for a moment in a venomous cloud and then drifted off across the lake.

Altor was relieved to discover he had not lost his grip on the silver sword. He looked around. 'Caelestis?' he said. He twisted from side to side in the water, scattering spray in a large arc, as he scanned the cavern in the dim light.

But there was not even a trail of bubbles to show where his friend had gone under.

As he looked around in panic he became aware of a green light in the murk. It was the talisman that had hung around the skeleton's neck. It was sinking back to the lake bed, drifting away and down like thistledown on the breeze. Near it, having smashed the boat and found no victims to feast on, the phantom broke apart into tatters of vapour. The vapour seethed and swirled, coiling into the water as it was sucked back into the talisman.

Altor stared at the fading green light. As his eyes penetrated further into the gloom he could see a large shape moving under the water, thrashing from side to side like the tail of an enormous fish. But it wasn't a fish. What was it?

He was about to turn and swim away when something broke the surface of the water. A silver-buckled boot with miniver trim.

'Caelestis!' called Altor.

Caelestis' foot kicked wildly and then was snatched back under again. He was in the throes of a desperate struggle with something in the water.

Altor cried out although Caelestis had no hope of hearing him: 'Caelestis, no! Leave it! You'll drown!'

He launched himself towards the glow, swimming downwards with all his strength. Caelestis had obviously tried to retrieve the treasure. Now his fingers were locked on the emerald, his arm caught in the bars of the cage as it bore him inexorably down into the depths.

Drifting mud made a dark cloud over the lake bed. As Caelestis sank into it it was as though he was being blotted out of existence. Altor saw his friend's face outlined in green light against the blackness just below him—eyes wide with panic, hair snaking like seaweed, bubbles gushing out of his mouth as he tried to scream.

Caelestis' free hand drifted up. Altor knew he had one chance. He made a grab for the hand and their fingers touched...

Eight:

Imragarn

Caelestis became aware of several things: hard rocks under his head, a crushing weight on his chest, and a bitter taste like grit in his mouth. It took him a few moments to realize that this meant he was still alive. He sat up and immediately vomited black water all over his waistcoat.

When the spasm in his guts had finally passed, he lay back with a groan. Somehow he had reached the far shore of the lake. Nearby stood something that looked like a large block of ice or glass. At the head of the shore a tunnel led further into the Battlepits, a faint light twinkling at the end of it.

'You're an idiot,' said Altor's voice near to him. 'A greedy idiot. You just had to have that talisman.'

Caelestis tried to speak and had a coughing fit instead. After it had passed he managed to say weakly: 'It was so close. But I got my arm caught in the cage. I had the emerald in my hand.'

Altor interrupted him. 'How do you feel?' he said coldly.

Caelestis eased himself back into a sitting position. Altor was crouching nearby, carefully drying his sword with a scrap of cloth. His short broom of hair was plastered down across his forehead in soggy honey-coloured strips.

'I don't think you need to worry about rust,' said Caelestis in a miserable voice. 'Whoever heard of a magic sword rusting? Where's my cloak, by the way?'

'It's difficult enough to rescue a drowning man while hanging on to one's sword,' said Altor. 'Something had to go, and I'm afraid it was the cloak.'

'You lost it in the lake?' Caelestis gazed bleakly out over the water where, to make matters worse, he now noticed his fine hat drifting half-sunk across the dark ripples. 'I don't believe it. Do you know what that cloak cost?'

'About as much as your waistcoat?'

Caelestis looked down. The pale silk of his shirt was streaked and torn, and the waistcoat itself was drenched in bile. Something resembling a fleshy barnacle was sucking at one of the purple jewelled button. With a sigh he ripped the waistcoat off and cast it into the lake.

'That's that, then. I might as well just lie down here and die, because things can't get any worse.'

'Don't be stupid,' said Altor. He got up and crunched across the pebbles to examine the block of ice. Beyond, against the rear wall of the cavern, was a bronze shrine flanked by fiercely burning braziers.

'Come and look at this,' he said.

Heaving a sigh, Caelestis got wearily to his feet and ambled over. After one look at the block of ice he was leaning forward intently, all complaints and discomforts forgotten.

'There's somebody in there..!'

The figure of a warrior clad in leather armour was just visible in the murky heart of the ice. He had his back to them. Altor walked around to the other side, where a gauntleted hand protruded from the block. It seemed that someone had chipped away at the ice in order to get at the warrior's sword.

'This is recent,' said Altor, running his fingers over the grooves in the ice.

'Maybe another of the champions passed this way. He might have lost his own sword in the lake.'

Altor touched the hand. It was cold, but not stiff as death should have made it. 'This fellow might still be alive.'

'You want to thaw him out?' muttered Caelestis, nodding towards the nearby braziers.

Altor strode over to the shrine and hefted one of the braziers. The flames trailed a plume of crackling gold in the dank air.

'Hold on a minute,' protested Caelestis. 'What's the point? The guy's got no sword to take, and I don't fancy any of his clothes.'

'He might be another challenger like us.'

'So?'

Altor began to position the other brazier. 'So he might be able to tell us something useful.'

'He might be dead,' grumbled Caelestis. Seeing that Altor was not to be deterred, he went on: 'Look, I know you're from a monastery and no doubt you've sworn to help those in need, but don't you think this is carrying charity a bit too far? While we're wasting time here, the other champions are getting further ahead.'

Altor set his jaw in a stubborn expression. 'You go on if you want, but I'm not leaving him here. Even if he is dead, he deserves better than to be left forever in a block of ice.'

Seeing that further discussion would be futile, Caelestis merely shrugged and sat down for a rest.

Once Altor had moved both braziers closer, the ice was soon melting. The block emitted strange snapping and creaking sounds as it shrank. Using a large rock, since he did not want to damage his sword-hilt, Altor smashed away until he had freed the man frozen within. From the tooling on his leather armour to the lashes on his lightly closed eyes he was perfectly preserved, as though all the time he had been encased in ice he was merely sleeping.

'He's going to fall over in a minute,' observed Caelestis.

Altor dropped the rock and placed his hands gently under the man's arms, surprised to note that the braziers were also drying out the water on the man's clothes so that it came off him in waves of steam. As the ice subsided, the man's full weight fell onto Altor and he grunted with the effort. He glanced across at Caelestis. 'Are you going to give me a hand?'

Caelestis brushed disconsolately at some mud that worked into the plush fabric of his trousers. 'It wasn't my idea to thaw him out in the first place,' he said sourly.

Then the last of the ice slid away and the man's full weight collapsed completely onto Altor. Although he was braced for it, the young monk was nevertheless caught off balance and found himself toppling back onto the pebbles. For a moment he lay there pinned, unable to get the leverage to lift the man off.

'He's heavier than he looks,' he grunted.

Caelestis reluctantly ambled over and helped to lift the inert body so that Altor could wriggle free.

'Stop groaning,' grumbled Caelestis. 'You were only winded.'

'I didn't groan,' panted Altor, getting to his feet.

They both heard it then: a distinct groan from the body lying amid the chunks of melted ice.

Altor knelt and felt the man's brow, then dragged him nearer to the braziers. 'He is alive!' he cried excitedly.

The man's eyelids fluttered open. Wisps of steam were still coming off his clothes as the heat from the braziers gradually warmed him. His long hair hung across his face in a lank curtain. In the leaping firelight it gave him a demonic appearance.

He turned his head and slowly looked around. As the focus came back into his eyes he turned in the direction of Altor and Caelestis.

'What happened?' he said, his voice croaking slightly. A shiver rippled through his body but then he took a deep breath to bring it under control. When he next spoke his voice was steadier. He looked calmly at the two young adventurers. 'The last thing I remember is my old chum Fashmar getting killed by that frost wizard. Then he flung a spell at me...'

Altor quickly filled him in while Caelestis looked on sceptically.

The man listened and shook his head slowly. 'Then I have been frozen here for almost a decade,' he said in a low voice. 'I came into the Battlepits with several companions. We were the champions of Magus Laglor. You didn't find any others like me, then..?' He glanced along the shore.

Altor shook his head. 'You were the only one.'

The man slumped for a moment, overcome by a stab of grief, then he looked up. 'My friends, I owe you my life.'

'Who are you?' said Caelestis in a tone that made no effort to disguise his hostility.

Altor glared at him, but the stranger managed a weak smile. 'Your suspicions are understandable, young man. The Battlepits are no place to forge a friendship. But rest assured that Imragarn of Achtan does not forget his debts.'

'That is your name, then? Imragarn?'

'He has said so, hasn't he?' demanded Altor, embarrassed. 'Where are your manners, Caelestis?'

He waited for Caelestis to apologize. Caelestis said nothing. After a moment, Imragarn got unsteadily to his feet, shrugging as if he did not mind Caelestis' open distrust. He looked between the two glowering youths. 'There is an expression in my country: manners are best kept next to a ready sword. I will earn your trust, my friends; I have no right to demand it.'

Caelestis kept his sceptical frown, but he said: 'Anyway, what do the rules of the contest say about this kind of thing? I suppose you'll have to join us, but are you now one of Balhazar's champions like us, or are you still working for Magus Laglor?'

Imragarn mustered a half-smile. 'Neither or both, for all it matters to me. When I came down here nine years ago I was full of dreams of gold and glory. Now I'll be glad just to get out alive.'

'There's only one route,' said Altor, pointing to the passage at the head of the shore. He led the way towards it and the others followed. Caelestis was careful to lag behind Imragarn where he could keep an eye on him.

The walls of the passage were smooth stone, and at the end was a vestibule in front of huge double doors. There was one curious feature about these doors. The carvings on them, which showed a gladiator locked in bloody battle with a dragon, were upside down.

'I heard a legend about this...' began Imragarn. He shook his head in confusion. 'No, it's gone. I feel like I've been dreaming... there's so much forgotten.'

Caelestis had no patience for listening to the man's rambling. He stepped forward and helped Altor push the doors, which swung back to reveal a long hall lit by glimmering chandeliers.

But the hall too was upside down.

Stunned by the sight, the three advanced along the ceiling between two rows of chandeliers that stood like huge bronze mushrooms. The candles set into them trailed feathery nimbuses of light that hung down in defiance of gravity.

Then they saw that their footsteps disturbed dust on the ceiling that fell up past them, trickling off towards the floor high overhead. It wasn't the candle flames that defied gravity. It was the three adventurers themselves.

'That is because you are the intruders here,' said a voice in answer to the thoughts of all three of them.

A light blossomed at the far end of the hall, where a thin figure sat on a monumental throne of swirling-veined marble. His robes spread around him like a pool of molten gold and his skin was a rich ebony black, his eyes sparkling star-bright in the gloomy vastness of the room.

And he too sat upside down. The three adventurers began to feel as if they had wandered into a dream.

'You have done well to come so far, though you are not the first,' the robed figure said. He seemed to be speaking barely louder than a whisper, but either by magic or a trick of the hall's acoustics they heard every syllable clearly.

Caelestis was the first to speak. 'Who are you?'

'I have no name. I guard the gateway to the lower level, where you must now go.'

'Why are we..?' Altor hesitated, shrugged. 'Why are we upside down?'

'The normal laws of nature are inverted here. You are halfway to the other world. But my only advice is to put all such questions aside. Logic will not serve you in the place where you must now travel.'

He reached out towards them and a moment later they felt a

tingling sensation crawl across their skin.

'What's happening?' cried out Imragarn in sudden alarm.

The other two turned and stared aghast as his image blurred, becoming ghost-like in front of their eyes. Then they realized that the same thing was happening to them. Slowly they began to slip down into the stone under them, feeling the solid surroundings only as a faint chill against the skin.

'Have no fear yet,' said the figure in the golden robes. 'This spell of mine will not harm you. It is what lies ahead that you should fear...'

Nine:

The Chasm

If the robed figure had any more to say it was lost as they submerged in stone. It was like sinking through thick tar at first, soon fading to no more than the breath of a slight cold wind. For a brief time there was nothing but a cocoon of darkness around each of them, the silence of an indefinite void all around.

At last they emerged from the rock into open air. Solid once more, they fell lightly to land on crude stone steps. An up-draught from below brought a stifling dank heat on which they could taste burning sulphur.

Imragarn clasped his hands to his shoulders and shivered. 'I thought I had only imagined you rescued me... that I was back in the ice...'

Caelestis recognized the tinge of panic in the man's voice. He did not entirely trust Imragarn yet, but there was no doubt his fear was genuine. 'in this heat?' he said, mopping his brow.

Imragarn gave a weak smile and Altor cast an approving glance at his friend. Caelestis' joke had stopped Imragarn from going into shock. For all his faults and fancy ways, the young thief was a good judge of men.

Nodding ruefully, Imragarn visibly pulled himself together. 'You must think me a pretty feeble ally.'

Altor laughed. 'Look at us—bedraggled, covered in lake mud. Hardly the grand heroes that Magus Balhazar would want representing him!'

'He'll want his money back if we don't get a move on,' said Caelestis.

'Not that he paid us in the first place, mind you.'

The three started to make their descent. The steps soon emerged onto a perilous ledge that snaked down the back wall of a vast underground cave. They looked out, awestruck, at the unearthly panorama before them. The cavern stretched away for two kilometres or more and the ceiling was a hundred metres high in places, supported by giant basaltic pillars that soared up into the dizzying gloom. The basin below was the crater of a dormant volcano, and a deep red glow illuminated the cave from volcanic geysers that spluttered and gurgled lava through cracks in the cave floor.

'We must be right under the city foundations,' said Altor, and the thought of the sorcery that kept the ravenous volcano in check took their breath away.

'The power of the magi is...' Caelestis paused, at a loss for words, 'much more than I imagined,' he finished somewhat lamely.

'It's nothing compared to the power of the True Magi who preceded them,' said Imragarn. 'Remind me to tell you about them later when we're relaxing over a pint of ale.'

Caelestis smacked his lips.

'Save that talk of ale,' said Altor. 'We need to keep our wits about us—now more than ever.'

Here and there from rents in the rock ceiling, trickles of noxious liquid sprayed down. The smell told them that those were the outlets from the Keep's sewers, and the volcanic fires burned with a resentful green light whenever one of these streams hit them.

The bottom of the crater, far below the ledge, rolled with a greenish white mist that made it difficult to see anything but the splutter of red fires. Three pinnacles stood out, islands in the sea of fog. The first of these was joined to their ledge by a narrow bridge. It was barely more than a metre wide, and there were no rails to hold on to. One slip would be enough to cast a person into the gorge, where a torrent of evil-smelling water flowed roaring below the mist.

Across the bridge, a soot-blackened temple could be seen atop the first pinnacle. A group of foul hags capered out onto the terrace in front of the temple and began to jeer at the three adventurers as they wended their way down the ledge.

'A welcoming party?' muttered Caelestis.

'No, look,' said Imragarn, pointing above them.

A host of winged dirges were swooping down through the foetid air. Altor reached for his sword as the sinister shapes began to wheel around in the air currents, but Imragarn put a calming hand on the younger man's shoulder.

'They won't attack,' he said quietly. 'They're scavengers.'

Ignoring the shrill cries of the black-winged dirges, they continued on until they stood on the wide shelf of rock leading on to the stone bridge. Across the deep gorge the ugly hags looked on and jeered, one of them throwing handfuls of a soft substance at the adventurers. Fortunately her aim was short of the platform.

Altor was at the front; he would have to go first. As he stood steeling himself to take the first step a voice boomed out into the abyss. He looked up and noticed a huge gargoyle head carved into the cave wall near the roof, its mouth moving in time with the ebb and flow of the strange sounds. He fancied he heard words in the rumbling noise, a voice intoning: 'Face those who wait for you in death.'

Altor shook his head and tried to fix his concentration on the task ahead. He stepped out onto the bridge.

A gasp behind him made him look back. A shimmering energy barrier had sprung up, preventing any possibility of retreat. Altor turned round and squared his shoulders. 'Right then,' he muttered under his breath, 'let's get it over with.'

He took a step forward. The gargoyle head spoke again: 'Arise from ashes.'

Altor looked around again, perplexed. It was only when he turned back to the matter of crossing the bridge that he realised the gargoyle's words had not been addressed to him. A figure was gradually taking shape ahead of him on the bridge—a hulking berserker in a rotting chainmail vest. He lifted his warhammer with arms that looked bloodless and dead. A flicker of red fire from a spurting geyser illuminated his face. The eyes were cloudy like pearls, the face just a tattered cobweb of decay.

'The winner shall have life,' groaned the stone head.

The berserker grinned and stepped forwards. He said in a thick voice: 'Ja, dearest foe. Here's where we change places.'

Altor, his sword already drawn, was puzzled. 'Dearest foe? I will gladly fight you if I must, but tell me why I should know you.'

'You do not know me. Our weapons have never clashed before this day, but I owe your blood-line a debt of hard hatred. I am Beorn Smith-hammer, slain by your father twenty long years ago. Now I will have my life.'

Altor was so surprised he momentarily forgot the perilous situation he was in. Raised an orphan at the monastery, he knew nothing of his parents. 'My father? You knew my father? Then tell me—'

His words were cut short as Beorn swung the hammer towards him in a bone-breaking arc. Acting on reflex, Altor dodged and struck out with his sword as the berserker was recovering his balance. Beorn stood teetering, but recovered and brought his hammer up hard towards Altor's face. Altor tried to step back, managing to avoid the blow, but tripped and fell on one knee. He looked up to see the tunnel of a mostly empty rib-cage and above him Beorn's ivory-smooth arms were raised to bring the hammer smashing down on his defenceless head.

In a last desperate move, Altor rammed his sword up inside the undead warrior's chest and into his head, twisting as he went. Beorn gave a scream that was visible as a trembling of his exposed vocal cords. Altor drew back the blade, ready to strike again, but its magic had severed whatever spell kept Beorn alive. He slumped forward, the hammer plunging into the soupy depths below.

The body stayed swaying on its feet like a broken puppet. A kick from Altor tumbled it off the bridge, where it vanished in the haze. And with it, he realized with a sense of sorrow so strong it felt like physical pain, went any hope of finding out more about his father.

Altor reached the other side and stepped onto the terrace. The hags glared at him, and one of them threw a handful of dung, which thankfully missed. He turned back to watch the others cross.

Imragarn was hesitant, so Caelestis stepped boldly out next. Since childhood, when he had been nurtured by some of the craftiest burglars of the Coradian lands, Caelestis had been used to leaping across city rooftops and scaling drainpipes. He had no fear of heights. Heedless of the long drop, he danced a precarious jig. The hags gasped and clapped their hands in glee, clustering at the brink of the gorge in their eagerness to see him fall. Caelestis windmilled his arms in mock terror. The hags clutched each other, barely able to contain their excitement. Then he recovered his balance and strolled effortlessly on, laughing when he saw the hags turn away and spit with disappointment.

Suddenly a rumbling voice dampened his high spirits.

'Come from death,' commanded the gargoyle head. In answer to its summons a shadowy figure materialised on the bridge ahead of him. It stepped forwards, and the ruddy light of the volcanic jets showed a man in a brocade gown, carrying a metal-shod staff. He had a jewelled patch over one eye, and the other was milky and sightless.

'Hurondus,' boomed the gargoyle head. 'Your dearest foe wishes to cross the bridge. Prevent this, and you shall be restored to life.'

'My dearest foe,' echoed Hurondus venomously. 'This is where we conclude our vendetta at last.'

'Vendetta?' replied Caelestis, shaking his head. 'I have never set eyes on you...'

The old man's milky eye seemed to gleam. 'Three years ago I was arrested and executed for one of your crimes. Three years I have waited for a chance to repay you.'

Caelestis snorted in protest. 'Then surely the one you really want revenge on is the magistrate who convicted you? It's hardly my fault if he got his facts wrong. Also, although I have admittedly committed a few illegal acts in my day, I've never done anything that would warrant execution. The magistrate was unduly harsh!'

'Babbling youth!' cried Hurondus in anger. 'Do you think I will waste my opportunity to be avenged?'

'By all means take your revenge,' said Caelestis with an easy shrug of the shoulders. 'But not on a blameless young chap like myself. Hurondus, use your new lease of life—or undeath, or whatever—to seek out that magistrate. It was his bad judgement that cost you your life, so—'

He was cut short by a screech of hatred. Hurondus raised his staff, snarled an incantation, and a gout of green flame went hurtling towards Caelestis.

Altor and Imragarn, on opposite ends of the bridge, saw the tumbling mass of flames. It struck where Caelestis was standing and exploded in a brilliant green light. The glare was so bright they had to shield their eyes.

When Altor looked back his heart froze in horror. Except for the blind wizard the bridge was now empty.

Caelestis had been burned to ashes!

Ten:

The Face of Death

Hurondus tapped his way forward, swinging his staff in front of him. When he found his foe was gone his shoulders began to shake with mirth and a horrible gravid cackle reverberated around the rock walls. He advanced slowly to the edge of the bridge, a brooding presence wrapped in his own thoughts of triumph, while Altor and Imragarn could only stand paralysed in shock.

As Hurondus's staff probed into the gulf, a hand suddenly shot up from under the bridge and grabbed the end. Hurondus gave a croak of surprise and began another spell. He hand pulled sharply and Hurondus flipped over and cartwheeled into the void. Somewhere deep in the white wreath of mist, his final spell exploded in a pale burst of green light.

Caelestis nimbly hauled himself up from under the bridge. The hags, annoyed to see him survive, hissed and emitted foul odours as he skipped across to join Altor.

'You gave me a nasty shock,' said Altor. 'I thought you were a goner.'

'What, and leave you to take all the reward money for yourself?' Caelestis grinned in sheer relief. 'You can't get rid of me that easily, my friend.'

Altor looked across to where Imragarn stood wavering. He called out in encouragement, but Imragarn seemed not to hear him over the dull reverberating roar of the river below.

The hags brayed with laughter, sputtering phlegm over their cyanic lips as they rubbed their hands in vicious merriment. Sensing Imragarn's fear, they anticipated a tragedy.

This time they were not to be disappointed. Imragarn edged nervously out onto the bridge. He was a stocky man, not light on his feet at the best of times, and his nervousness made it worse. As he neared the middle of the bridge, the gargoyle boomed its summons: 'Relinquish the grave.'

In answer to the summons, tendrils of mist licked up from the clouds below the bridge. They thickened to form a hazy pillar ahead of Imragarn, then gradually subsided to reveal a dark cowled woman of majestic stature. She stepped towards the trembling figure of Imragarn, and by her gait the gruesome goddess was revealed: Hela, Queen of the Dead, Ruler of the Afterlife.

'Imragarn,' Hela said in a voice to chill the blood. 'I am the one you must face, for I am Death and you belong to me.'

Imragarn started to raise his hands in defiance, but they were shaking. Caelestis and Altor saw him take a deep breath and try to draw himself up to his full height as he stared the dread Queen full in the face.

'No,' he said, 'I defy you. I have been given a second lease of life. Why should I give it up?' He shook his head violently.

Hela smiled, but it was the smile of Death. 'You were torn from me and I have searched long and hard for you in this place. You and I belong together...'

She reached for him with lean white hands. 'I know you have been so lonely without me,' she said softly, and her voice was like the whisper of dry wind through the hollows of a skull.

'No!' cried Imragarn, and turned away from the apparition, his eyes screwed up in pain.

'Imragarn!' called Caelestis. 'Don't listen to her! You're with us and you are alive!'

Altor put a hand on his arm. 'He's beyond hearing you,' he said gravely.

Imragarn was rooted to the spot, his whole body quivering with the conflict that raged inside him. He looked towards Hela, the emotions on his face flickering between defiance and resignation.

Hela moved to embrace Imragarn and he let out a roar and thrust her away with all his strength. She dropped out of sight over the side of the bridge. Stunned, Imragarn went to the edge and stared down into the void after her, but there was no sign of any falling form and when he turned around Hela was again standing there.

'There is no escaping me, Imragarn,' she said with surprising tenderness.

He looked at her for a long moment, and then his trembling stopped and he allowed her to enclose him in her arms. The look on his face now was one of adoration. To Caelestis and Altor the Queen of Hell appeared only as a grinning monstrosity of bone and gristle. But perhaps Imragarn could also see her other aspect—no monster, men say, but a goddess beautiful beyond belief.

The two of them faded away, leaving the bridge stark and empty.

Altor and Caelestis were both too stunned to speak.

At last Caelestis managed a wisecrack: 'That's as close as I ever want to get to Death if I can help it!' But his tone was too hollow to sound flippant, and there was a slick of nervous sweat on his brow.

'I'll light a candle in the Abbey for Imragarn's soul when I get home,' said Altor. 'He deserves that much, at least.'

The show over, the hags were wandering back to their cauldrons in front of the ruined temple. Altor nodded towards them. 'Do you think we could get anything useful out of them?' he said dubiously.

Caelestis strode up to the hags. 'Well now, weird sisters, what are you doing?' he asked, putting on a bold voice even though the sight of their warty faces and snaggle-toothed gums was enough to make him feel like retching.

The hags looked up and grinned. With their skin creased by long long years and their eyes like tiny blighted holes it was like looking at a row of rotten pumpkins.

'Just our cooking,' said one, clattering the lid of her pot aside. A bilious aroma shot up Caelestis' nose, bringing tears to his eyes. Altor, catching a faint whiff that was still strong enough to strip paint, wisely hung back.

Another of the hags scuttled over and put a hand on Caelestis' bare arm. 'You're a tasty little morsel, ain't you?' she cackled. 'A bit on the scrawny side, though. Want a taste of this to put some meat on them bones?'

She proffered a ladle dripping with steaming gruel.

'Wait a minute,' screeched another, 'I don't think the seasoning's quite right.' She took a decomposing rat out of a pouch beside her and dropped it into the bubbling cauldron.

Altor decided things were getting out of hand. 'Can you tell us if anyone else has passed this way?' he asked in a stern voice.

The hags dissolved into a hideous parody of girlish giggling, clutching each other for support. 'Lots. Many. A number beyond counting,' tittered one at length.

'Today?' pressed Altor.

'Oh, you mean recently? One there was from far away, from a land where the sun rises and finds the birds still a-slumber.'

'She means the Orient,' realised Caelestis. 'That would be the warlock, Icon or whatever his name is.'

'If you say so, laddie,' said the hag. 'And there were two scurvy knaves who resisted all our blandishments—no, not you two. Your friend's too strait-laced to be called a knave, and you're both too young and wholesome to be called scurvy.'

Not liking to receive flattery from one so ugly, Caelestis said hurriedly: 'And was that all?'

'All but a single swordsman who survived the bridge crossing where his comrades died. He helped us with our cooking...'

She glanced significantly at one of the cauldrons. Altor and Caelestis, following her gaze, thought to see an unpleasantly recognisable titbit rise to the surface momentarily before sinking back into the stew.

Altor turned uncomfortably and looked out across the fiery vastness of the cavern. 'Time we were on our way.'

They moved away, but one of the hags hobbled eagerly after them. 'Don't you want to know what the future will bring?' she demanded.

'This all started because I was fool enough to get my fortune told,' grumbled Altor. 'From now on I think I'll let the future come to me.'

'Very philosophical,' said Caelestis, 'but right now I wouldn't mind a bit of forewarning. Go on, then, grandma.'

She extended a hand that looked like a badly mummified chicken claw. 'Don't you know the routine? You've got to cross my palm first with a bit of old silver.'

Caelestis took out the silver obol he had taken from the sarcophagus beside the lake. 'I thought you gave that to the boatman?' cried Altor in astonishment.

'Nah. Oh, I showed it to him all right. Then I palmed it and slipped him a copper penny instead. He never knew the difference, and I thought this might come in useful.'

'More likely you thought you could sell it to a coin collector!' snorted Altor.

Caelestis shrugged. 'Easy come...'

He flipped the coin into the air. The hag's hand shot out and caught it. After making sure she had really been given the silver obol and not a substitute coin, she grinned up at Caelestis and said, 'One question, then. Make it count.'

Altor was about to say they should think about the question very carefully, but by that time Caelestis had already opened his mouth. 'What's the worst thing we must face?' he asked.

The hag scratched at her chin thoughtfully. In the process she detached a hairy wart which she popped into her mouth and sucked on with due deliberation. 'Hmm, I will have to give you two answers, for there are two dangers you must face. One is the giant Skrymir, whom Magus Zyn will ask you to resurrect. However, to face that you must first cross the canyon of lava on the back of the dirge-man Droctar, and since he was transformed from a man into a dirge as punishment for his wickedness you would be right to expect treachery from him.'

'I wonder if we're any the wiser now,' said Altor. 'Oh well, let's be on our way.'

'Wait!' cried the hag. 'Have a sip of this tasty broth to set you up for the tasks ahead.'

She held out the ladle that she held in her other hand. Caelestis peered at it, not liking the way sticky bubbles rose to the surface where they popped like overfed grubs. 'What is it?' he asked.

'Just a nice broth.' Her eyes hardened. 'Go on, drink!'

Without a word, Altor wrested the ladle away and tossed its contents over her. There was a hissing and the wretched hag took a step back, wailing as thick clouds of grey steam rose from her. In seconds she had dissolved leaving just a puddle of noxious slime. The other hags screamed and spat in rage, but as Altor and Caelestis moved away they scurried over to crouch around the puddle. Caelestis didn't turn away quite quickly enough to avoid seeing them start to lap up the slime.

'If she was so good at telling fortunes,' said Altor, 'I wonder why she didn't see that coming.'

'I guess you only get the future you pay for,' said Caelestis. 'And she looked like a skinflint.'

Skirting the temple, they found a narrow ridge leading off to another pinnacle. A ruined shrine painted in lurid red firelight squatted atop it, the pillars tilted and surrounded by fallen masonry. Beyond, pits of lava seethed and sputtered like the beacons of hell.

Altor and Caelestis exchanged a glance. The ridge looked precarious but with nowhere else to go they set out along it. The knife-edge path forced them to go slowly, Altor in the lead with his sword glittering icily in the furnace-red light. On either side, steep rock slopes plunged down into sulphurous mist. Ahead, the ruined shrine loomed in the ashen murk.

A scrabbling noise caused their pulses to quicken. Dislodged rocks went clattering off the path and were caught with muffled splashes by the lava below.

Caelestis looked back to see a flash of white against the gloomy red haze. Hunched shapes were clambering onto the path behind him. They moved like giant insects, stalking with gnarled limbs splayed, pallid bodies agleam in the fiery light. In their hands they carried shards of flint sharper than any sword.

More of them poured onto the path up ahead. Altor and Caelestis were surrounded.

Eleven:

The Lake of Fire

The figures resembled insects, but the truth was even more frightening—they were men whose humanity had been stripped away from them by terrible fanaticism. As they came closer Caelestis saw they were cultists who he recognized as worshipping the demon-god Balor. They were said to cut out their own tongues as a mark of devotion. Their bodies were daubed with funereal grey corpse-paint, their faces hidden under white skull masks which transformed them into impassive angels of death.

The nearest of the cultists lunged forwards. He seemed to uncoil from slow motion into in a grey blur. The dead silence of the attack almost caught Caelestis off guard. He ducked just in time, drawing his sword as the cultist's flint knife whirred through the air over his head.

'Trouble,' said Caelestis as he speared the cultist on his sword.

'Same here,' replied Altor with equal economy. He was facing a man who must have been the cult champion, a burly warrior whose swollen muscles, flexing under his grey body paint, made him look like a corpse fished out of the water after drowning.

The man lowered his masked head and charged. Altor raised his silver sword, but the man took no notice. He came bearing down the path, eyes gleaming fanatically in the dark sockets of his mask. It looked like he would happily run straight onto the blade as long as he could get his hands on Altor's throat.

Altor knew that if he let the first foe grab him he would swiftly be overwhelmed by the rest. Instead he crouched, then straightened up with all the strength in his back and legs just as his foe leaped at him. The big man was thrown over Altor's head, went sailing above Caelestis as well, and cannoned into the other cultists who had attacked from behind. He lay sprawled for a second, looked around in amazement, and was just getting his bearings when Caelestis stepped forward and drove a sword blade through his neck.

'Don't you think I've got enough of my own to fight back here as it is?' said Caelestis over his shoulder.

'I thought you'd like a look at that one, seeing as how he was so big.' Altor dispatched another cultist and was relieved to see bright red blood on his blade. Under the paint they were just living men after all.

The cultists fought with a ferocity and deadly speed born of fanaticism, but the same eagerness to serve their god made them careless. They seemed to welcome death, almost running to impale themselves in their eagerness to fight.

The rest of the battle was brief, fought in grim silence. Altor and Caelestis only realised it was over when no more white robed madmen came flinging themselves headlong out of the smoke. Slapping footfalls on the bare rock told them that one or two of the cultists, at least, valued self-preservation more than the demands of their god.

'You're injured,' said Caelestis.

Altor glanced at the ribbon of blood running across his hand. There was a red rent in the padded leather of his sleeve. 'Luckily flint makes a straight cut. I'll sew it up when we stop for a breather... What are you looking for?'

Caelestis was peering down the slope. Tendrils of yellow mist crept across the grey rocks, but Altor could see nothing else. 'I was just thinking those cultists must have had a lair nearby.' Caelestis pointed. 'See that little cave?'

Edging carefully down the pebble-strewn slope, he approached the cave. It was really no more than a rough fissure between two boulders. Volcanic fumes spewed out continually, drifting downwards to add to the swirling fog far below. Caelestis was about to give up and return to the ridge where Altor was waiting when something caught his eye. Holding his breath, he reached inside a little way and his hand encountered something hard and round. It was a copper tube covered with green patches of corrosion.

Caelestis scrambled back up the slope to show his find to Altor. 'What do you think?'

'It looks like a scroll-case.' Altor took the tube and with some effort managed to unscrew the end. Carefully he extracted a piece of brittle parchment.

'What does it say?' asked Caelestis eagerly.

'It's written in Dakkandi, a debased variant of the language used by the True Magi in olden times. Er, let me see... "Skrymir, who was great—"'

'Skrymir? That's the giant the witch told us about.'

' "...who was a giant," then. "An enemy..." something... "slain and dismembered by the magi's representatives."'

'Or champions?'

'Yeah, that's more like it. 'Lord Zyn..." Magus Zyn, that is... something I can't read... "and therefore consigned to remain in fire." That's all I can make of it.'

'The value of a good cloister education,' said Caelestis. 'I'll bet you can work out compound interest as well.'

Altor smiled. 'It doesn't take an education to realise that there's no profit in hanging around here. Let's take a look at that shrine.'

They advanced along the ridge and between the ruined columns of the shrine. On the walls hung marble skulls, one gleaming white, which the volcanic mists had stained the colour of old tobacco. A copper dish stood in the centre of the floor, gleaming in the occasional spurts of fire from outside. Around it lay several discarded white robes and death-masks, but the remaining cultists had by now fled.

From the back of the shrine led another narrow path above a near-vertical precipice. They wended their way along the ridge, which rose like the sharp backbone of an ancient dragon out of the indistinct cavern floor. A murky sea of mist sat in the hollows below, now and again illuminated by lightning gouts of red fire.

The path brought them at last to a high-walled crater where a tall pylon of rugged stone rose above the steam. Entering the arch at the bottom, they climbed the staircase within until they emerged on a high balcony near the top of the pylon.

From here they had a spectacular view across the cavern, a view that showed them in one glance the immense size and frightening beauty of the Battlepits. Lit by flickering sparks and sporadic bursts of fire, it was like a depiction of the dying hours of Hell at the far end of eternity.

The crater swept away beneath them towards spires of sharp broken rock. In the middle distance was a plain carpeted with swirling mist where standing stones poked up from the ground like serried fangs. Beyond the plain, barely visible in the glimmering light, stood a squat atoll of dark rock.

'That's where the Emblem of Victory is,' said Altor with firm conviction. 'I sense it.'

Caelestis looked out across the fiery vista with a sinking sensation. 'It's a long way yet.'

'It is,' nodded Altor. 'I suspect everything we've faced up till now is nothing compared to what lies ahead.'

'A cheerful sentiment. Let's snatch a few minutes' rest while we can, in that case.'

They settled down with their backs to the stone battlements and few a few minutes neither said anything, each lost in his own thoughts. Caelestis looked up to see Altor examining the cut in his arm. It was a deep cut, still bleeding. Caelestis took out his handkerchief. It was a square of fine Khitan silk with a gold C embroidered on it. It had cost him twenty silver florins from a tailor in Ferromaine and a few hours ago he would have counted it as one of his most cherished possessions. He hesitated a moment and then handed it to Altor. 'Here, use this.'

Altor looked up. 'You're sure?'

Caelestis nodded and pushed it into his hand. 'Go on, while you've still got some blood to lose.'

Altor bound the handkerchief tightly around his arm. It looked awkward to manage with one hand, but he acted as if he was used to that kind of thing so Caelestis didn't interfere.

Altor looked up thoughtfully. 'We didn't really get off on the right foot, did we, Caelestis? I know I thought you were a good-for-nothing wastrel at first—'

'Remind me never to ask you for a testimonial!'

'No, what I mean is that it turns out you're okay. I want you to know that I count you as my friend.'

'A funny time to mention it,' said Caelestis. 'You can buy me that tankard of ale later, though.'

Altor finished knotting the handkerchief. 'Well, I just wanted to say it now in case the worst comes to the worst.'

'Worse than what?' Caelestis stared at him as though he were demented. 'Since this morning I've been half-drowned in a lake that smelled like bilge water, I've thrown up over my waistcoat, lost my hat and cloak, my shirt's in such a state that I might just as well tear it up to make bandages, and my boots are so badly scuffed that I'd be ashamed to give them to a beggar! On top of all that, I submit, death would almost be a blessing.'

Altor seemed hardly to have heard his friend's outburst. 'I was thinking about the old musician.'

'Who?'

'The one who gave me the pommel stone.'

'The pommel stone? Oh, right. Look, I'm sorry about that, Altor. Obviously if we'd known each other I'd have thought twice before robbing you, but you were a complete stranger at the time.'

'Oh, I'm not blaming you. Not much, anyway. But I made the the musician a promise. '

'If it turns out you can't keep your promise on account of getting killed, then I think he'd understand.'

Altor abruptly got to his feet. As he flexed the bandaged arm Caelestis saw him wince, but rather than saying anything he just handed him the silver sword.

'Ready to go on?'

Altor nodded. 'We're in this contest to win, aren't we?'

'Certainly. I need my share of the prize money for a new suit of clothes.'

'Well, we won't win anything sitting on our backsides.' With a decisive stride Altor led the way back down the stairs.

They found a chamber whose huge wooden doors had fallen in, the hinges long since corroded by the volcanic exhalations of the place. The two friends stepped past and emerged again into the hot acrid air. Directly ahead of them, in the centre of the crater, lay a lake of boiling mud.

Altor pointed along the crater rim. 'Maybe we could get around that way?'

Caelestis' eyesight was sharper. 'No. See there, where it's collapsed? And on the other side of the crater too. We'll have to somehow get across this mud.'

They walked down the steps in front of the pylon until the lake of mud was only a few metres below them. The heat rose of it in breath-stealing waves. All across the surface, bubbles blistered the surface and the slow swirl of current showed like creases in molten pitch.

'I'm open to suggestions,' said Altor hopefully.

Caelestis looked around thoughtfully, then his glance fell on the collapsed doors of the pylon and a sudden inspiration spurred him into action. Scrambling back up the steps, he bent and ran his fingers over the wood. Once the coating of dust was wiped away, the doors showed a dark reddish-black sheen.

'Yggdras hardwood,' Caelestis murmured to himself as Altor came up.

'What does that mean?'

Caelestis looked up at his friend with a broad smile. 'It means we can get across the lake! I'm talking about a raft, Altor.'

They set to work improvising a raft using a broken section of the huge wooden doors. Another shaft of wood, presumably the bolt that once held the doors shut, would serve as the oar. Between them, the two young adventurers manhandled the raft down the steps and pushed it out onto the lake. Globules of sizzling mud clung to the sides but the wood was buoyant enough that the upper surface of the raft stood well clear of the lake. Altor and Caelestis tested their weight on it. The raft lurched and a little mud spilled over the sides, but once they had planted themselves in the middle it seemed steady enough.

'What do you think?' said Altor.

Caelestis watched the boiling mud the way a canary studies a cat. It looked hot enough to bake the flesh off their bones in seconds. But there was no other choice. Even if they were to abandon any hope of winning the contest, they still had to cross this lake to get out of the Battlepits.

'Let's do it,' he said.

Taking the makeshift oar in both hands, Altor began to scull across the lake. It was hard going. The mud sucked at their raft, allowing only the most sluggish motion, so that after only a few yards Altor's shoulders were already aching with the effort. Still, he was keenly aware that the mud was scalding hot and he had to take care not to splash any onto their skin.

A flurry of motion drew their attention to the ridge encircling the crater. They squinted through the heat-haze to see two Coradian warriors whom they recognized as the champions of Magus Kito. The Coradians seemed to be caught in a frantic battle, but at first it was not clear what they were fighting. Balanced perilously on the rim of the crater, one of the two dropped his sword and pressed his hands to his face. A plume of white flame rose into the red gloom and the man's cry of agony came faintly across the bubbling lake. He teetered for a moment on the brink, then plunged back into the mud where he writhed briefly and went still. Slowly the mud pulled his body down out of sight.

The other Coradian turned, swinging his sword desperately but without hope. Seeing Altor and Caelestis on their raft, he called out. The words were lost over the hungry bubbling of the mud.

Again a spout of fire showed above the crater's rim. The Coradian gave a shriek and tumbled down to join his comrade in death.

Altor resumed paddling with redoubled effort. The raft bumped against the far edge of the crater and the two leapt off, clawing their way up the slope of loose rock until they stood on the rim.

Caelestis glanced back in time to see indistinct fiery shapes gliding across the mud. As he shifted his position, his feet dislodged a few stones which went rattling down the slope a fell with dull plops into the seething mire below. Huge bubbles of sulphur gas rose and broke on the surface. They were followed by heads that emerged grinning with maws of flame. They reminded Caelestis of blazing Hallowe'en effigies—only these were not carved from pumpkins. They were formed of living fire.

Twelve:

The Dirge Man

The creatures rose up the slope as though weightless, flickering talons extended towards the two friends. Those wide hot grins suggested that killing the Coradians had not assuaged their murder-lust—they were still eager to sink molten fingers in frail flesh, to boil human blood in a clutch of flame.

Caelestis stood frozen in horror as the fire elementals glided up towards him. He could feel the waves of heat rising off them like hot breath on his skin.

Altor caught his arm and pointed to an incline leading off from the rim of the crater, down towards the cavern floor. Caelestis nodded mutely, the numbing spell of fear broken, and they set off at a sprint.

The incline was gentle at first, but soon became a steep slide of fused glassy-smooth lava. With the fire creatures behind them there was no time to look for footholds—they careened down, sliding, half falling, sobbing for breath but not daring to stop even if they had been able to on the steep path.

The floor of the cavern loomed ahead. Altor and Caelestis came off the slope at a run and, unable to keep their footing, pitched to the ground in gasping heaps.

Warmth rose palpably through the ground from volcanic furnaces in the heart of the earth. Caelestis found it quite comfortable, despite the hardness of the rock where he was lying. His body ached with the day's exertions, he was weary, and all he had to get up for was yet more danger and discomfort. How pleasant it might be just to lie here instead, rest a little...

Altor shook him roughly. Caelestis sat up scowling resentfully. 'It's no use, I can't run any further. You'll have to leave me.'

'We're safe,' said Altor, shaking his head. 'Apparently the fire demons don't like to stray too far from their mud lake.'

It was true. The fiery creatures lingered for a short while on the outer slopes of the crater, then turned and flitted back to where the pylon showed dimly in the haze above the ridge.

Caelestis breathed a sigh of relief. 'What I find it hard to believe now,' he said, 'is that I got into all this merely to avoid landing up in Kalugen's jail. Why? It's a comfortable enough jail. There's bedding—admittedly just a bundle of rancid straw, regular rations of cold gruel and rainwater, and looked at in an optimistic light the place is at least as good as the worst peasant hovel. Surely that would have been infinitely preferable to the Battlepits!'

'Oh, stop griping,' laughed Altor. 'We must be nearly at the end. If the witches were telling the truth, there's only the Oriental wizard ahead of us.'

'And Droctar the dirge man and Skrymir the giant still to contend with,' Caelestis reminded him. 'If indeed they were telling the truth.'

He got to his feet and gazed ahead. Smoke and mist shaded the perspectives of the cavern into an eerily artificial scene. A desolate plain of earthen mounds and standing stones separated them from a swart atoll that reached nearly to the roof of the cavern. At the very top of the atoll, bathed in a stark grey white light that seemed to emanate from no natural source, stood a proud banner emblazoned with bezants of shining metal.

'The Emblem of Victory!' cried Altor. 'We've reached our goal, Caelestis.'

'Not quite,' said Caelestis dryly.

He pointed as a slow stirring in the hot air moved aside a bank of vapour. They had not seen it at first, but there was a wide chasm stretching right across the plain from one wall of the cavern to the other. Mist seethed thickly within it, white and luminous, so that for a moment they had the impression of standing on a high mountain peak and gazing down at the clouds. The only way to reach the atoll where the Emblem stood was to cross this chasm.

They looked in vain for a bridge. Just as failure seemed inevitable, spiralling down out of the haze of steam came a creature with a dark hairy body and wide wings like leather sails. As it swept closer they saw it was like the dirges they had encountered earlier, but this one had an almost human face.

'This'll be Droctar, no doubt,' said Altor out of the corner of his mouth. 'Remember what the witch said—he's not to be trusted.'

The dirge man drew up, clawing the air with his wings so that he hovered just overhead. At close inspection his features looked very human indeed, but it still came as a shock when he called out in a croaking voice: 'Ho, this gulf presents itself as a daunting obstacle to one who lacks wings, would you not agree?'

Caelestis took umbrage at the creature's mocking tone, but he bit back on the retort that jumped to his lips. The dirge man might be their only hope of getting across the chasm. It would not do to antagonize him.

He forced an affable smile. 'Perhaps you can help?'

The dirge man settled on a mound of stones nearby, flexing his enormous grey wings as if glad of the rest. For a while he sat deep in thought, then suddenly raised his head and said brightly, 'I could fly you across.'

'We'd be very grateful,' said Altor.

'And your gratitude would be most precious to me,' said Droctar. 'Do not think I'd count it of little worth, oh no! But all the same, there would have to be a proper, real and material remuneration into the bargain. Without it, any transaction between us would seem imprecise and unsatisfactory.'

'With those wings you must be a strong flyer,' said Altor warily. 'If you can fly with half the gusto you put into speech, in fact, you ought to be able to lift a house. No doubt, then, you can carry the pair of us?'

'Pah!' cried Droctar. 'Do you mean to say I am verbose?

Unnecessarily prolix? It is only that I feel every bargain should be transacted with perfect clarity.'

'We admire and value the precision of your bargaining,' said Caelestis. 'My friend only seeks reassurance. The chasm is rather deep, after all.'

'You need not concern yourselves with its depth,' said Droctar with an odd cracked laugh. 'It is full of molten lava, you see.'

'As long as you don't drop us,' said Caelestis, 'neither its depth nor its contents need concern us, surely.'

'Quite so.' Droctar stifled a yawn. 'As to payment, then...'

In reply Caelestis held up his hand. By luck a geyser shot up a glorious spurt of white-hot rock nearby, causing the gold ring to scintillate.

Droctar gave a gasp of admiration and sat forward. 'An extraordinary treasure!' he croaked, avarice swamping all reason. 'Give it to me and I shall convey you across the chasm at once.'

'Exactly my own sentiments,' agreed Caelestis, 'with this minor modification: convey us across the chasm and then you will get the ring.'

Droctar hid a sullen look which he managed with difficulty to twist into a smile. 'You drive a hard bargain,' he declared, 'but I should expect no less from those who venture so far through the Battlepits. So, then, it is agreed—'

Caelestis raised a finger. 'Not quite. You are forgetting the 'abrogation clause'.'

'Either my vocabulary or my legal expertise are deficient,' grumbled Droctar. 'I have never heard of any 'abrogation clause'.'

'Essentially it is the option to change your mind, thereby invalidating your right to receive the goods or services agreed under a transaction.'

'I see. So if you invoke the 'abrogation clause' I should simply drop you in the chasm?'

'Exactly. And if you should do so then it means you're under no obligation to take the ring.'

Droctar scratched the spray of bristles that corresponded to his beard. 'It hardly seems worthwhile including such a preposterous clause.'

'Under current law it is essential if the agreement is to be considered valid!' insisted Caelestis.

Droctar threw up his arms. 'Very well.' He fluttered down to where they stood and waited while they looped their arms around his neck. Then, stretching his great wings wide, he clambered up into the steamy air.

They sailed out over the chasm, the frothy clouds sliding past below. Under them they caught flashes of lava-fire as volcanic spouts spat constantly. Roaring wind currents rose, slamming them to and fro at random, but the dirge man was used to the crossing and manoeuvred with a bizarre elegance.

Halfway across, to the surprise of neither Caelestis nor Altor, the question of payment came up again.

'I have been searching for the proper way to broach this next subject,' announced Droctar, 'but I am at a loss to do so without some compromise of delicacy. Therefore I think it is best to be quite candid. If you do not give me the ring now, immediately and at once, I shall loop over and drop you into the lava.'

Altor scowled, but he could not easily draw his sword while clinging to the dirge man's neck. In any case, what use would a sword be now? He glanced at Caelestis, who warned him with a wink not to do anything hasty.

'Wouldn't you like to know why this ring is so special?' he said to the dirge man. 'It's because it contains a magical imp—behold.'

So saying, he called the Faltyn out of the ring. It appeared in the air beside them, clad in bedchamber silks and lounging on a cloud in the form of a huge white pillow. 'You again?' it said acidly. 'I thought you'd be dead by now.'

'Not quite,' replied Caelestis, trying not to think how near to the mark the creature was. Keeping his eyes averted from the sheer drop into the abyss, he managed a calm tone as he said: 'Our friend

Droctar here is flying us across this chasm. As a matter of fact he hasn't always been the hideous winged monster you see now. Once he was a man—'

'Ho now!' called Droctar in a voice tinged with suspicion and the first stirrings of alarm. 'What are you up to?'

'—A man,' Caelestis pressed on, 'transformed by sorcery. I wonder whether your impish magic is up to the task of turning him back?'

The Faltyn glanced at the lava churning in the chasm below, then back to Caelestis with a sly grin. 'Of course; nothing could be simpler. You are asking me to do so now?'

'Wait!' cried Droctar. 'If I revert to human form we will all fall into the lava and drown.'

'It's the fate you intended for us anyhow,' said Altor, seeing now what Caelestis' plan was.

'Unless you'd care to invoke the 'abrogation clause', that is?'

'Yes! Yes! Just send away your genie. I want nothing to do with it or the ring.'

The Faltyn could not mask its expression of disappointment as Caelestis banished it back into the ring. 'Set us down here,' he told Droctar. 'And no more treachery, or you'll be ash and sparks within an instant.'

Whimpering in fear of his life, the dirge man fluttered down to land on the far brink of the chasm. Altor immediately leapt clear, whipped out his sword, and pressed it to the creature's belly.

'Devil!' he cried in outrage. 'I should run you through for such double-dealing.'

'Do so if you wish,' said Droctar drearily. 'It would merely be a release from torment. I am heart-sick of my punishment, and would as soon be dead as stay a monster.'

Altor had no taste for slaying a foe who did not fight back. 'Go,' he spat. 'Get out of our sight. You deserve the punishment the Krarthian magi chose when they put their spell on you.'

'Do I?' Droctar said as he took to the air once more. 'Perhaps as a man I was deceitful, but I was never so evil a creature as the magi have made of me. Farewell, then, mortals. If you survive the Battlepits you may discover why it is that the magi are princes of falsehood.'

He climbed into the air until the veils of white steam first blurred and then swallowed him up.

'What did he mean?' wondered Caelestis.

'Just a final spiteful remark to unnerve us,' said Altor. He turned and gazed towards the atoll, an indistinct grey shape beyond the mist-shrouded plain. 'Come on, Caelestis. Victory is at hand. We mustn't falter now.'

Thirteen:

Icon the Ungodly

They set out across the cavern. From time to time came the sounds of small scuttling creatures between the rocks, but they could see no sign of life under the dense white blanket of fog. Light came from the grey sparkling veins in the cavern roof, the streams of phosphorescent sewage leaking from above and the intermittent spouts of flame that vented up from deep under the earth. In one such blast, Caelestis glanced up at the peak of the atoll and thought he caught a glimpse of the Emblem of Victory limned in fire-red against the dark of the cavern roof. Then the flame flickered out and heavy darkness dropped behind the grey mist like a shutter.

They passed a stone monolith and, despite his eagerness to reach the atoll, Altor could not resist pausing to study the ancient sigils that covered its pitted grey surface. The sigils seemed alive with magical power, but it was power that was closed to Altor and Caelestis.

Altor traced them with his fingers. 'What do they say?' asked Caelestis curtly, impatient to reach their goal.

'Even the modern magi cannot read those runes.'

It was not Altor who had spoken. The two young adventurers turned to see a black-clad warlock standing only a few paces off, his silver-threaded cloak wrapped around armour of an exotic style. He had approached so suddenly and silently that he might almost have taken shape out of the mist itself.

'I know you,' said Altor warily. 'Icon the Ungodly.'

The warlock made no aggressive move but bowed with elaborate Oriental courtesy, saying, 'Some in these lands call me that. I am the champion of Magus Uru just as you, I believe, serve the cause of Magus Balhazar.'

Caelestis tucked his hand in his belt where it was reassuringly close to his sword. 'Are we the only ones to reach this far?'

'We are,' said Icon. 'The way has been arduous and fraught with peril. Many have fallen.'

Altor's upbringing at Osterlin Abbey now left him in a quandary. On the one hand he knew that a man dishonoured himself by anticipating treachery. On the other, his instincts warned him that the Battlepits were no place to give a stranger the benefit of the doubt. Uncertainly he drew his sword.

Icon looked at the blade of bright silver metal, a cold white thread in the dull red glimmer of the cavern. 'Is it my time to die, then?' he said wistfully. 'I can't defend myself from you. Most of my magic has been used up getting this far. So do what you must.'

Altor took a step forward, faltered, then thrust his sword back into its scabbard. 'Why should we slay each other for the magi's amusement?' he snarled bitterly. 'An alliance is permitted under the rules of the contest—and we still have to face the giant.'

'My friend is a guileless soul, which is to his credit,' Caelestis said to Icon. He spoke politely, but his tone was like sharpened flint. 'Personally I trust you no more than I would trust a starving fox to look after my chicken coop.'

'At least you are being honest, which is a good beginning between allies,' said Icon with the faintest of smiles. 'I shall try to win your confidence. As for the prize, we'll have to share it of course—but even a shared prize will make us all rich.'

Altor said nothing at this.

'My friend is infected with saintliness,' said Caelestis pointedly, angry at Altor for being so trusting. 'He wanted nothing of the prize, just a single boon from Magus Balhazar.'

Icon's smile broadened but became no warmer. 'Honour is merely another currency, like gold or gems. Shall we be off?'

'You first,' said Caelestis. Since he didn't like the idea of allying with Icon in the first place, he had no intention of turning his back on him.

They set off once more across the cavern, Icon leading the way. Altor fell back to speak to his friend in a lowered voice. 'I realize you don't approve, but teaming up is the best way to ensure we all survive.'

'In general principle that's true,' admitted Caelestis, 'but it often fails to hold in practice. For instance, consider the case of two mice allying with a snake. Mutuality of survival is not then guaranteed.'

Altor broke into a smile. 'You have a colourful way of expressing yourself, my friend.'

Caelestis was not to be mollified. 'Just keep your eye on this fellow. We must assume that he did not acquire his epithet of 'the Ungodly' because of a reputation for good deeds.'

Altor was about to reply, but the words vanished in his throat. He had caught sight of something remarkable in the mist ahead. A heavy basalt platform hung suspended in the air fifty feet above their heads.

Icon had noticed it too. Quickening his pace, he led them over. On the ground directly underneath the platform stood a bronze gong. Taking a small bronze mallet from a pocket in his robes, Icon went to strike the gong.

Caelestis caught his arm. He felt taut, powerful muscles below the black silk sleeve. He knew Icon could have broken his grip with ease, but instead he turned to face them with a placid gaze.

'First tell us what you're up to,' said Caelestis, releasing the hand that gripped the mallet.

'My studies warned me to expect this,' said Icon. 'Hence I scoured the western lands for this mallet, which is the only means by which we will be able to speak to the ghost of Magus Zyn.'

'The scroll we found said something about him,' Altor recalled. 'And the witch mentioned him too...'

'He was one of the True Magi,' said Icon. 'Much greater wizards than these modern upstarts who now rule Krarth, they were all slain in the eruption that destroyed the city of Spyte. Except for Magus Zyn, who had been so powerful that the other magi bound his spirit here in the Battlepits to prevent him from resurrecting himself.'

'Why disturb him now, in that case?' Caelestis challenged him.

'He understands how to deal with the giant Skrymir. We have to find that out before we can attain victory.'

Neither Caelestis nor Altor had an immediate answer to that. Caelestis was still suspicious, but while he was racking his brains to remember exactly what it was that the witch had told them, Icon had turned once more towards the gong. Before either of them could even think to stop him, he had struck it.

A deep note resonated in the air, building just beyond the range of hearing so that it was like being surrounded by a vast swarm of invisible bees.

They felt a tingling sensation, then watched in fear as incandescent gold sparks sprung from the gong to crawl around them.

There was a sickening jolt. The surroundings swum out of focus, altered, came sharply back into relief. Caelestis, who had experienced a very similar sensation earlier in the day, guessed at once what had happened: 'A teleportation spell!'

The other two did not need him to tell them. They could see plainly enough from the fact that they were now all standing on the basalt platform with a fifty foot drop to the cavern floor where they had only a split-second before.

Only Icon seemed unamazed. 'Of course,' he muttered to himself, 'it would not be seemly for Zyn to come to us when he could instead bring us to him.'

All three of them turned at once, not because there had been any sound but because they felt the presence of something cold and uncanny. A large jewelled coffin occupied the middle of the platform, and in the phosphorescent gloom they saw an old man rise from it, passing through the closed lid to hover candle pale in the air before them.

Even Icon stood dumbstruck until the ghost spoke, stirring the air with a voice reaching across a gulf of centuries.

'Magus Zyn I was, in life,' it said. 'Mightiest of the True Magi, as has been told, I would have ruled over all, but petty jealousies brought about my downfall. Foolish rivals slew my servant, the giant Skrymir, and though they lacked the power to destroy me utterly, they yet imprisoned me here. Here I have lain for ten centuries. Ten centuries! They have passed like the slow tread of Leviathan, like the measured rumble of the gods as they snore beneath Spyte. Ten centuries to plot and scheme... Now my plans for vengeance reach fruition—with your help.'

Caelestis glanced at Icon, who was nodding to himself thoughtfully. Altor stood with folded arms, glaring grimly at the ghost. 'Why should we help you?' he demanded.

'Behold the landscape of the netherworld.' The ghost swept its translucent arm to take in the mist-draped volcanic vista below. 'Cold rock lies heavy as the lid of a tomb; draped over it is a grave-cloth of dank mist. But underneath rage the very fires of the Inferno. So it is with me. I am dead, my mortal shell but ashes, but my spirit burns with the garnered ferocity of a millennial hatred. If you refuse me then it will count for but a flicker in the eternity of my existence, but I shall see to it that your suffering screams endure throughout all time.'

'Who's refusing?' blurted out Caelestis hastily. 'Sure we'll help.'

'It is well,' replied the ghost with a misty smile. 'The loyal servants of Zyn shall share in his glory, and you shall be rewarded above all others.'

'I don't like this,' said Altor under his breath. 'It's always a bad sign when a wizard starts referring to himself in the third person. Particularly a dead wizard.'

'I agree,' whispered Caelestis, 'but we'll have to go along with him for the time being, otherwise we'd be stuck up here.'

Icon cast them a hot sidelong glare. 'How can we serve you, O puissant lord?' he asked the ghost.

In answer it passed its hands over the jewelled coffin and the lid rose slowly into the air. They looked upon a mouldered skeleton that clutched a lump of fused rock in its broken fingers.

'My mortal form,' said the ghost wistfully. 'So long it has been since I tasted the musky wines of Asmuly or felt a scented breeze from off spring meadows... Take the stone! Take it quickly! I wish to wallow no more in memory of things forever lost to me.'

Icon stepped forward and took the lump of stone from the skeleton's hands, and the coffin lid slowly closed again.

He held up the stone. 'It looks like a fossilized heart,' said Altor.

'It is the heart of the giant Skrymir,' explained the ghost. 'He was destroyed by the True Magi, but he shall be my instrument of vengeance upon their heirs, these mewling modern upstarts who have usurped the ancient grandeur...'

The ghost flickered and seemed to grow larger and more tenebrous for a moment, then settled down to a cold hard radiance. 'Go towards the atoll. I have no interest in this petty contest; it is of no concern to me whether you take the Emblem of Victory or not. However, on your way to the atoll's summit you will pass through chambers where the sundered fragments of Skrymir's body lie—his massive legs, his rib cage, his arms and fleshless skull. Take them with you. At the summit, assemble them and place the heart I have given you in his dusty chest. Then stand you back, for the magic of Zyn shall roar forth from the cosmic interstices once again as it did in times of old. Flesh shall clothe Skrymir's yellow bones; his heart shall beat and warm blood shall course through his veins; his eyes shall open and behold this travesty of ancient Krarth, and to the upstart magi he shall mete out a most fitting fate.'

'We get the picture,' said Altor. 'How do we get down from here?'

The ghost raised its diaphanous hands. 'Make ready. My simplest spell will serve to return you...'

A stream of grey-blue light surrounded the three of them. The scene shifted and once more they found themselves on the plain below the floating platform.

Icon turned to resume the journey towards the atoll, but Altor caught his sleeve. 'Just a moment. You told us we needed Zyn's advice on how to deal with the giant, but from what he said it sounds like the giant is already dead.'

'And would have stayed that way if we hadn't got involved,' put in Caelestis more vehemently. 'Now we're supposed to put him back together! Come clean, Icon—you expected all this, didn't you?'

Icon looked thoughtful. 'It was why I came to take part in the contest,' he said after a moment. 'Do you think I would have travelled the whole width of the world merely for gold? The magi are untrustworthy employers at best, and I suspect their real purpose in holding the Battlepits contest is simply to relish the violent deaths of the losers. Rather than rely on the meagre gift that Uru chooses to give me for bringing him the Emblem, therefore, I prefer to ally myself with Magus Zyn and take the lavish reward of sorcerous power.'

'Ally?' said Caelestis dubiously. 'He doesn't regard us so highly. You heard his threats: we serve him or he'll send us straight to hell.'

'He'll value us right enough if we serve him well,' insisted Icon. 'In any case, the deed is done. Shall we stand here and bicker, or press on and take whatever rewards await us?'

'On,' said Altor, nodding. But he wore a dark frown now. He was beginning to share his friend's qualms about the mysterious Icon.

They trudged on across the blasted wasteland, the mist falling back in forlorn wisps as they reached the higher ground climbing to the atoll. It rose above them, a brooding monolith of hard black rock. On a ledge high above, they could just make out the tassels of the Emblem of Victory fluttering in the ghostly breeze that streamed around the summit.

A slope led up into a crevice in the base of the atoll, and passing through this they found a path winding up and around it like a helter-skelter. The way was steep, and none of them complained upon reaching a ledge where they could stop to rest.

Caelestis sat down wearily but Altor remained vigilant. He sensed danger. Looking around, he saw a reddish glimmer appear that lighted the outline of a small cave off the back of the ledge.

Icon had seen it too. Stepping smartly over, he reached into the cave and rolled out what at first looked like a small boulder. It was with a shock that the other two suddenly recognized the shape of a massive skull.

'It must have belonged to someone more than twenty feet tall!' gasped Caelestis.

As they stared at the skull in amazement, a groan issued from its jaws. Then it spoke.

Fourteen:

The Magi's Downfall

They all stood dumbstruck as the skull spoke to them.

'I was Skrymir the giant,' it said. 'Skrymir, who dared to challenge the True Magi. This was in olden times, before the Blasting which put mere apprentices on the ancient thrones. You think these modern lords of Krarth are mighty? The True Magi were wizards indeed! They blew spells that shrivelled my flesh into dust, they turned my heart to stone with their fierce glares, boiled my blood with their rage, cracked these old bones with shouted incantations.'

'Magus Zyn has sent us to restore you,' said Icon.

There was a long pause, so long that they began to wonder if they had only imagined the skull spoke, but then the voice boomed out again: 'Collect my bones together—this skull through which I now speak to you and the other sundered fragments you will find. At the summit join them together. Then I shall rise again and sweep away those capricious prattlers who now style themselves as magi! Give me life, mortals, and your reward will be beyond the dreams of avarice.'

The skull fell silent. After a moment, Caelestis said: 'Let's just roll it off the ledge and have done.'

Altor was in agreement, but Icon shook his head. 'We would never be allowed to leave the Battlepits. Zyn would summon us back with his magic and consign us all to hell. No, my friends, it is too late for second thoughts—we've thrown in our lot with Zyn, for good or ill.'

'If that is so,' said Altor reluctantly, 'I think it's certainly for ill.'

There was nothing more to say. They resumed the climb up the ramp with Icon rolling the huge skull. At the next ledge they found a rib-cage of colossal proportions hanging from a petrified tree. A large padlock attached it to one of the stone branches but at a harsh command from the skull, like the tolling of a great bell, the padlock fell open and Icon took the rib cage down.

At the next ledge was a roughly carved throne to which were shackled the giant's pelvic bone and skeletal legs. Again the skull spoke and the shackles slithered away, rustling their rusted links on the stone as they retreated into the shadows.

'Help me,' said Icon. 'I can't carry everything myself.'

Altor shook his head. 'I want nothing to do with it.'

'Me neither,' said Caelestis.

Icon sighed. 'I can't blame you for being afraid. You are young, and already you've experienced enough since entering the Battlepits to affright the bravest of men. But I urge you to steel yourselves, keep your nerve for just a little longer.'

'It is not fear that holds us back,' said Altor angrily, 'but reasonable doubt that this is the right course of action.'

'Maybe with a little bit of fear thrown in,' added Caelestis.

'How many times must I say this?' said Icon, his eyes suddenly narrowing as though to hide his innermost thoughts from them. 'If we fail to do what Magus Zyn requires of us we will rot here forever! We are allies, so I ask again: help me.'

'I wish you'd consulted with your allies before you struck the gong and got us into this,' said Altor curtly. Nonetheless, he lifted the massive bone legs across his back.

On the next ledge were skeletal arms affixed to shoulder blades like plates of ivory armour. One fleshless hand still wore a spiked gauntlet of iron. Despite his misgivings, Caelestis picked these up and the three continued up the atoll with their burdens of bone.

The slope levelled out. They had reached the summit at last. Barely a dozen paces away stood the Emblem of Victory, its metallic bosses and rich fabric bathed in the bright glare of a beam of light stretching up to the ceiling of the cave.

Caelestis had thought he would want nothing but to touch the Emblem and be conveyed to the surface, but now that it was within his grasp he paused and, setting down the heavy skeletal arms, turned to look back over the Battlepits. From this vantage point he could see the glimmering fires and phosphor streams, the blanket of mist and the hovering platform where Magus Zyn's coffin rested, the chasm where the dirge-man flew, a distant speck, and the pylon above the lake of boiling mud with the ruined shrine lost in the gloom beyond.

'We've come so far...' he said.

Altor rested a hand on his shoulder. 'Didn't you think we were going to make it?'

Caelestis remembered their conversation while Altor was binding his wounds on the battlements of the pylon. He smiled. 'Of course. I just didn't expect it to be so hard.'

'I was thinking of the others,' said Altor. 'Imragarn, those Mercanians, the guys on the crater rim, the rest of them... They gave their lives—for what? The chance of a bag of gold.'

'They were fools,' said Icon. 'Gold is nothing more than prettily coloured dirt. It is power that counts in this world.'

They turned to see him inspecting an iron frame that lay overgrown with brambles and half-hidden in the shadows behind the rock where the Emblem stood. 'This is the armature into which we must fit the giant's bones,' he declared with obvious satisfaction.

'I think it's time we abandoned that project,' said Altor.

Icon looked at him with unconcealed contempt. 'I can't believe I have to explain this yet again! If we fail to carry out Magus Zyn's orders we'll be punished. On the other hand, if we do as he commanded and rebuild the giant, our reward will be much greater than anything the magi could give us.'

'He didn't seem to me to be the sort to keep his promises,' said Altor, shaking his head.

'Forget about his threats, anyway,' said Caelestis. 'The moment we touch the Emblem of Victory we'll be transported to safety. If Zyn's power could reach beyond the Battlepits then he wouldn't need our help in the first place.'

Icon averted his face, stood sunk in brooding thought for a few seconds, then turned back with a sigh of resignation. 'No doubt you're right, my friends. Forgive my obstinacy. Let's join hands on the Emblem, then, and return to the surface, where we shall feast tonight in the best tavern in Kalugen's Keep. But first, Altor, I see that you are wounded and, since I still have a little magic left, let me cast a spell of healing so that we may all go to our victory banquet whole and healthy.'

Caelestis was about to cry out a warning but, whether it was needed or not, there was no time. Altor's hand went to his sword but Icon had already raised his hands and chanted a few words in his native tongue, a grin of feral mirth spreading instantly across his face. Instead of healing, Altor's wounds burst open under their bandages and he sank to the ground with a gasp of pain. The silver sword clattered on the rock beside him.

Caelestis whipped out his own sword. 'You surprised me,' he said.

Icon's grin turned to a sneer. 'How disappointing. I thought you, at least, were expecting this betrayal all along.'

'Oh yes. I just thought it'd be sooner.' He leapt forward in a long lunge that should have driven his sword-tip through Icon's heart, but the warlock caught the blade in the folds of his cloak and darted back, pulling his own sword from its scabbard as he did.

Caelestis glanced quickly at Altor. He could see blood soaking through the makeshift bandages, and although Altor was struggling to regain his feet it was obvious he would be out of the fight for a while yet. He turned back to Icon just in time to parry a slashing attack to the face.

'I don't think your colleague will recover in time to save you,' Icon taunted.

'Well, I could use the fencing practice anyway,' replied Caelestis, circling round to try and force Icon to the edge of the summit.

But the warlock had no intention of making it a fair fight. Swiftly drawing a glass phial from his robes, he flung it at Caelestis' feet. The glass shattered and a violet fluid splashed across the rocks, instantly turning to thick fumes. Caelestis covered his face at once, thinking the fumes to be poisonous, but Icon gave a peal of derisive laughter. 'I wouldn't do anything that obvious!' he jeered.

Caelestis tried another lunge only to find his feet rooted to the spot. He flailed his arms, off balance, and in doing so dropped his sword. Looking down, he saw that his feet were caught fast inside a tangle of violet tendrils that had sprouted out of the bare rock.

Icon stepped forward and kicked Caelestis's sword out of reach. 'You did very well,' he said, 'but now it's over. And I have won.'

Altor had crawled over to a boulder and used it to pull himself into a sitting position. The ground around him was covered with blood from his opened wounds. Half-fainting from pain, he glared at Icon and said through gritted teeth: 'You didn't do any of this for the Emblem, did you? Or even for anything Zyn's ghost can offer. It was Skrymir's skeleton you were after all along.'

Icon nodded. 'Caelestis was right when he said that Zyn's power can't reach beyond the Battlepits. I intend to resurrect the giant and use him to make myself overlord of Krarth. Then I shall plunder the old libraries of the True Magi which their modern heirs have left to grow dusty with neglect. I shall become the mightiest wizard the world has ever known—mightier than Zyn, mightier than any of them.'

While he spoke, Icon was laboriously fitting the huge bones of the skeleton into place on the iron frame. Gradually a towering figure took shape, the fleshless remnants of the long dead giant. When everything else was completed to Icon's satisfaction, he fetched the massive domed head and lifted it up to the top of the frame. As he did, a cold dry wind whipped up around the atoll.

'Skrymir's soul is returning from the dead.' Icon smiled in satisfaction, though there was a nervous gleam in his eyes.

Caelestis had been wrenching desperately at the violet tendrils, but they were as strong as steel cables. He gave up the effort and glanced over to his friend. Incredibly, Altor had managed to get to his feet and retrieve his sword, but he was reeling with weakness and looked on the point of passing out. With his left hand pressed to the blood-soaked bandage around his thigh, he took a faltering step towards Icon.

Icon noticed the movement out of the corner of his eye. He began to turn, his hands already coming up instinctively to fashion a spell.

'Icon,' said a voice from behind him. 'Icon, it's Magus Zyn.'

Icon looked round. There was no-one there. Too late he realized he'd been tricked by Caelestis's ventriloquism. He conjured a gout of red fire in his hand and, whirling, drew it back to hurl at Altor.

The young warrior-monk had no other choice. He was too weak to run. Calling on his last reserves of strength he threw the silver sword -

The red flame dropped from Icon's fingers. He stared down in amazement at the blade protruding from his chest. His face was ashen and contorted with pain but, instead of falling, he reached down and pulled the weapon out, flinging it away as though the silver metal burned him.

'My magic shall sustain me until I have time to heal,' he groaned, forcing each word through a snarl of agony. 'But I must retreat to lick my wounds, and so you've thwarted me. Be warned: Aiken of the Utayama remembers his foes...'

Glaring coldly at them as blood trickled from his mouth, he spat the words of a spell of transformation. Rapidly his body dissolved into a red mist which seeped down the side of the atoll.

Caelestis felt the tendrils loosen from around his ankles. Tugging free, he hurried over to Altor in time to stop him from falling over.

'It's okay,' said Altor, swaying back onto his feet. 'The pain's going now. Icon's spell must have been broken.'

'I think he had to use all his magic just to keep body and soul together. Even so, you've lost a lot of blood.'

Altor shook his head to clear it. 'Can't worry about that now... The giant...'

They both looked at the skeleton hanging on its iron frame. Already patches of skin were sprouting like fungus on the dry bones. A spark of life glimmered deep in the sockets of the skull.

Caelestis could only think of one way to counter such sorcery. He held up his ring and called on the Faltyn. It appeared in a burst of blue smoke, its habitual expression of vacant insolence turning at once to undisguised terror. 'Send me back!' it cried.

'Send you back? I want to stop the giant returning to life first!'

The Faltyn took no notice. 'I do not care to involve myself in the affairs of Magus Zyn and his creature. Put me back in the ring, I beg you!'

The skull's jaw dropped open to suck in breath. 'First use your magic,' insisted Caelestis.

'I have no magic strong enough! No, I must depart at once! Here, take back the gem I extorted from you earlier—only let me go back!'

So saying, it pressed the pommel stone into Caelestis' hands. Seeing that argument was futile, Caelestis dismissed it with a scowl.

Strong sinews spread across the huge skeleton. The sagging skin filled with muscle. Altor staggered forward to retrieve his sword. Caelestis saw that it was futile. They could do nothing against the power of the giant—if his magic ring was not sufficient then neither would the silver sword be. Then, as he felt the pommel stone in his hand, he remembered the third of Larisha's gifts...

He fished it from his pocket: the sparkling orange gemstone that Larisha had described as the last breath of a dragon-lord.

Caelestis glanced up at the frame. The giant was almost whole. There was just time. Darting forward past Altor, he popped the orange gem into the giant's gaping mouth.

Skrymir flexed his arms. The iron frame now formed a suit of armour around his rock-muscled body. His beard sparkled with icicles, his eyes burned like frost. He rose slowly to his feet and the ground shook as he moved. Towering high as the shadow of a great glacier, he raised his head towards the cavern roof and gave a shout of exultation that shook the very bedrock.

'Skrymir stands once more upon the earth!' he cried. 'The rime of the northland fills his thews. The land reverberates to his battle-roar. Let the would-be magi who crouch upon the old thrones of Krarth beware—they shall not see another dawn, for the sky then shall be washed with their blood.'

His voice was as terrifying as thunder, as wild as a primeval storm. Altor and Caelestis saw that they could never hope to battle such a creature. To him they were less than ants. Small wonder that the Faltyn had fled in abject fear. If the magi in the city above knew of Skrymir's resurrection, they must be trembling now.

The giant turned towards the flickering beam above the Emblem of Victory and gave a roar of both delight and hatred. Climbing to the very peak of the atoll, he knocked the Emblem aside and stood bathed in the beam for an instant. As the spell took hold, he shimmered and faded.

'He's gone to the surface, where he'll wreak havoc no doubt,' said Altor. 'Somehow I don't think we can expect a reward.'

'Well, at least I got your pommel stone back.' Caelestis handed it to him.

Altor looked at it a moment, then closed it in a strong grip. 'When I think of everything we've been through for this...'

'Was it worth it, I wonder?'

'It was to me,' said Altor. 'All I wanted was to honour my vow to a dying man. Now I think that perhaps I should have agreed to complete his quest, as he asked me first, for I believe it to be an honourable one. There is nothing in the world worth more than honour, Caelestis.'

'Except for food, wine and a hot bath.' Caelestis chuckled bleakly.

'What now?' said Altor, glancing at the Emblem of Victory. 'I don't relish what we'll find above, with Skrymir marauding through the Keep.'

As if in answer a distant spout of flame flared indistinctly through the mist.

'Well, we can't stay here,' said Caelestis.

They reached for the fallen Emblem and together carried it to the peak. Weariness weighed them down after their long ordeal, but they knew it wasn't over yet. Somehow they still had to escape from Kalugen's Keep before Skrymir took his bloody vengeance on the city and all within it.

They exchanged a look. Altor was grimly determined. Caelestis cracked a smile. 'Here goes nothing,' he said.

The beam shone starkly around them and they disappeared.

An instant later they found themselves in the Great Hall of the magi. The scene that greeted them was one of carnage and confusion.

Skrymir was pacing the length of the hall spreading destruction in his wake. Bodies lay crushed and moaning, a horde of frantic courtiers and servants clogged the exits, screams came from all sides as the angry giant ripped blocks of masonry from the walls and hurled them at the crowd.

Several of the magi had collected their wits enough to flee, disappearing off to the safety of their distant citadels along inter-dimensional corridors opened by magic in the air.

Others had not been so quick to react. Among the dead were the pulped corpses of Magus Uru and cruel Magus Kalugen. Magus Venzor lay not far off, groaning piteously in his death-throes. His body had been crushed when Skrymir stepped on him.

The giant paused in his violent rage and fixed the occupants of the hall with a look of blizzard-fury. 'To live again!' he thundered. 'To turn about the yoke of death and place it upon the magi's necks! This is all I dreamt of in my centuried sleep. So now, you magi, quake in fear. Bolt the gates of your citadels. Marshal your armies and your puny magics. Skrymir strides the world once more, and this time his iron-shod feet shall tread your mortal bodies into the mire!'

Altor took Caelestis' arm and pointed towards an exit, intending that they should slip away in the confusion, but then they both felt Skrymir's dark gaze on them. The feeling was like the first frost of a cruel winter. Slowly they turned to face him.

'Skrymir was raised from his grave by mortal hand,' murmured the giant menacingly. 'Is this meet? Should the proud Lord of Jotunheim endure such shameful obligation? No! You two must take my place in death, and bear a message from me to the Queen of Hell. Tell her that before another day is spent I shall be sending her a host of souls—enough to swell the borders of her realm!'

He took a heavy step along the hall, provoking the watching courtiers to fresh bleats of terror. But Altor and Caelestis stood fast, defiantly facing the giant.

'You're a frost giant, isn't that so?' said Caelestis.

Skrymir paused, confused. 'My home is a land of hard winds and ice-rimed peaks, of—'

'Yeah, yeah.' Caelestis covered a yawn and turned to Altor. 'He's a frost giant all right.'

Altor didn't know what Caelestis was planning, but he had learned to trust his friend's wiles. 'He certainly talks enough for twenty giants,' he said scornfully. 'But talk is cheap.'

Skrymir roared and pounded his foot on the floor. The walls shook and masonry dust rained down from cracks in the roof. 'By the blood of the old gods!' he snarled. 'For this insolence your deaths will be painful indeed.'

'You're full of hot air, Skrymir,' said Caelestis.

Skrymir was enraged beyond words. He stooped to snatch Caelestis in his hand, but was prevented by an enormous belch that caused his to clap his fingers to his mouth. A wisp of steam curled from between his lips. His expression turned from anger to puzzlement and then dismay.

'What's the matter, giant?' taunted Altor, remembering now the magic gem that Caelestis had tossed into Skrymir's mouth.

'I think it's something he ate,' said Caelestis.

Skrymir clutched at his stomach and gave vent to a long scream of agony that shook the building and forced everyone to cover their ears. Altor and Caelestis looked up, and in the wind that issued from the giant's throat they saw red sparks that blazed with all the fury of a dragon's last breath.

Then Skrymir fell, smashing to the floor with such force that the marble flagstones cracked and people were thrown off their feet. Through the clouds of stone-dust thrown up they saw him gave a short convulsive spasm as the burning flame exploded within his belly. A creature of frost, he could not endure the power of heat and flame. The smell of brimstone and charred flesh filled the air, spreading in a cloud of black smoke. Even as they watched, the fire spread through the huge body and within seconds it had been reduced to ashes. This time not even Skrymir's bones remained.

Altor and Caelestis had seen so many horrors that day. Now they felt drained, bone-weary. Numbly they turned away from the smouldering cinders that marked a giant's shadow on the broken floor. Pushing their way to the exit through the press of ashen-faced guards and courtiers, they emerged from the choking clouds of sulphur-smoke into the clean raw wind of early evening.

Fifteen:

The End of the Beginning

'You don't have to come,' Altor was saying. 'Just tell me where Janirus lives.'

Caelestis shook his head. 'I think it's better if I show you the way.'

Powdery snow had begun to swirl down out of the charcoal sky. The square was deserted, the street lamps unlit. Kalugen's soldiers were in confusion. With their master dead, they were more interested in looting his palaces than in patrolling the byways of the Keep. All sensible citizens stayed barred inside their homes.

Altor and Caelestis stepped into the lee of a building, out of the biting wind. 'It's just up ahead,' said Caelestis.

Altor nodded and, gripping the pommel stone in his left hand, started along the street. The lantern in his other hand cast a blurry beam of light through the snow.

Caelestis caught his arm. 'Wait, I've got to explain something first...'

Altor glanced back. The firm set of his jaw betokened impatience, but then he relaxed. He had gone through so much to deliver the harpist's stone; another few minutes wouldn't make much difference.

'Okay,' he said.

Caelestis, who was never normally at a loss for words, chewed his lip pensively. 'The old man who gave you the stone,' he said at last. 'He said you were to give it to Janirus.'

'I already told you that.' Altor was getting impatient again.

'Yes, yes. But think back, Altor. What did he say exactly?'

Altor cast his mind back to that night in the forest glade. Incredible to think that it had been only a few weeks ago—so much had happened since then. Altor felt that he had left his monastery as a boy and would be returning a man.

'He said the stone was part of a sword...' he remembered. 'He wanted me to unite it with the other pieces. There were five pieces in all—no, that's not it. There were five foes—'

'The Five?' said Caelestis with emphasis.

'Yes. Does that mean anything?'

'You know the comets that streak nightly across the sky above Krarth? People call them the Five. They are stars of ill omen. Some say they're the ghosts of five of the True Magi.'

Altor nodded. 'I believe that may be what the harpist was trying to tell me. The Five are planning to resurrect themselves, the way that Magus Zyn arranged for Skrymir to live again. The harpist wanted me to find the parts of the Sword of Life and stop them...'

His voice trailed off and he looked up into the night sky. The comets were hidden beyond the veils of snow and cloud, but their baleful presence could still be felt. Altor realized now that he'd been aware of it since arriving in Krarth.

'What about Janirus?'

Caelestis's question broke him out of his reverie.

'The harpist said that if I couldn't take on the quest I should deliver the pommel stone to Janirus. 'Then you'll know,' were his last words. Know what, I wonder?'

'Why couldn't you take on the quest?'

'How can I?' Altor waved the hand holding the stone in a vague gesture of helplessness. 'My duty is to get back to my monastery.'

'But you went through the Battlepits to get the stone back. That was a quest, wasn't it?'

'I'm doing what I said I would. I'm going to pass it on to Janirus and that's where my involvement ends.'

'You don't sound all that certain.'

Altor scowled, annoyed at himself. He had planned all along to give the pommel stone to Janirus and then be done with it. Now that he was about to do that, why was he having second thoughts?

He set off along the street. Caelestis hurried to catch up. 'I think you'd better prepare yourself for a bit of a shock...'

Altor wasn't listening. The street ended in a small cobbled square with a water pump in the middle. Thin spines of ice dripped from the mouth of the pump. Behind, on the wall of a building was something that Altor took to be a door.

'Is that where Janirus lives?' he said.

Caelestis didn't answer.

Altor stepped past the pump and raised the lantern. He could just make out a word written high up on the wall. It was weathered, worn away by time, half faded back into the ancient stones from which it had been carved.

'Janirus...'

What he had taken for a door was simply a sheet of rough bronze fixed into the wall. He put down the lantern and touched the bronze. The frost had made it so cold that his fingers stuck to the surface. He pulled them away.

Caelestis came over and used the sleeve of his coat to wipe away the frost. Altor looked again. His own image gazed back at him, dim and dark as if seen through smoked glass.

'Janirus is the name of this spring,' explained Caelestis. 'It was also the name of a wandering priest who came to the Keep a long time ago. Apparently had intended to obtain a position at Magus Kalugen's court, but he found he could not turn a blind eye to the cruelty and injustice here. He preached against Kalugen, who had him arrested and put to death. The next day a freshwater spring appeared on the street corner where he was executed. Right where we're standing. Kalugen was too frightened of such holy magic to do anything about it, so the pump was put here and people can come to get clean water whenever they want.'

Altor nodded thoughtfully. 'And the bronze mirror?'

'I don't know who put that up. I've come to get water here myself, and in daylight you can clearly see yourself in the mirror. But as to what it means—who can say?'

'I think I know.' Altor stared at the pommel stone, glinting dully in the faint lantern-light. He came to a decision. Looking up into the night sky, he called in a strong voice: 'Hear this oath, you ghosts of the old magi. I, who have been entrusted with this stone, shall find the other parts of the Sword of Life. Therefore heed this, your only warning. Remain among the dead; do not seek to re-enter the world and pollute it with your ancient depravities. If you try to descend once more to the mortal vale, Altor of Ellesland will be waiting for you. You shall not prevail!'

To this challenge there was no answer, unless you counted the mirthful howling of the night wind. On a deserted street in Krarth, two youths stood under the brooding sky and felt the weight of destiny.

TO BE CONTINUED